LADYSMEAD

LADYSMEAD

JANE GILLESPIE

St. Martin's Press
New York

Library of Congress Cataloging in Publication Data

Gillespie, Jane, 1923-
  Ladysmead.

  I. Title.
PR6069.H38L3   1983   823'.914   82-16773
ISBN 0-312-46433-9

First published in Great Britain by Robert Hale Ltd.

First U.S. Edition
10 9 8 7 6 5 4 3 2 1

One

A clergyman of small independent income, who has seven daughters, can not be hopeful of marrying them all to great advantage. If his parish lies in the remote countryside of the borders of Lancashire, with little society, he can not be too hopeful of marrying them at all.

The Reverend Thomas Lockley, whose circumstances these were, was not greatly concerned with the difficulty. He was a studious and reclusive man, diligent in the performance of his duties, stern in his principles and apparently contented with his lot. It was upon his wife that the burden of their daughters' future weighed; already she had deplored her inability to give her children the education she felt they deserved; that she saw no way of settling them suitably in life did weigh considerably upon her.

But almost as soon as the eldest Miss Lockley reached marriageable age the burden was fortunately lifted. Mr Lockley had from time to time, to augment his means, taken pupils into his house, to benefit from his own erudition. One of these was a young James Merton, whose family held estates in Suffolk. He had been recommended to Mr Lockley by an old Oxford acquaintance; he was a lively and well-disposed boy, ready to admit that his preoccupations with horses and cricket during his schooldays had unfitted him to enter university life on a level with his fellows. During his time with the Lockleys he worked willingly, and was as grateful for the severity of Mr Lockley's tuition as he was for the motherly care of Mrs Lockley. When he had left Oxford he returned to visit the Lockleys, and found that there had matured in himself, as well as academic aptitude and the responsibility of manhood, a tender affection for the eldest Miss Lockley. This she returned; they were married, and he took her away to Suffolk.

Happy as they were, the young Mrs Merton naturally missed her family, and her sisters were invited to visit her. In the course of these visits, very soon two of them formed acquaintance that led to matrimony: Miss Anne married a solicitor in Ipswich, and Miss Priscilla married another friend of her brother-in-law's whose family owned a prosperous saddlery business in London.

Sad as she was to have three of her children so far from her, Mrs Lockley was gratified that they had been so well established in the world. Anne and Priscilla were her third and fourth daughters; her second, Sophia, returning from visits to Suffolk still unattached, her mother comforted as well she could: "I could not have borne to have all my dear ones at such a distance. Soon enough, you will leave us too. Let me – and your father – have the pleasure of your company for as long as we may." It must have been a pleasure indeed for Mrs Lockley to have female company, while the youngest girls were still children, and the neighbourhood offered scanty society for her. Sophia was fond of her mother and enjoyed the position of her mother's chief companion and confidante; but when, during the following summer, she and the fifth daughter Mary went to stay with their father's sister in Liverpool, and *Mary* engaged the affections of a young naval lieutenant, Sophia felt the cage of spinsterhood beginning to enclose her. To have three younger sisters married implies an accretion of years to one's own age however unjustified by chronology.

"I shall never marry now," she told her mother with tears of despair.

"Certainly you will," Mrs Lockley assured her.

"But I am growing *old*. No man will look at me. It is unfair. I am as pretty as the others – And I am sure I never make myself disagreeable –"

Mrs Lockley said with firmness: "You are all good-looking, good-natured girls, and it is only chance that has set your sisters before you. As for growing old, let me hear no more such nonsense."

"But Mary is not yet seventeen. And I am twenty-three this month –"

"It so happens that my daughters have married unusually young, and it need not be so in every case. Please do not entertain any suspicion of jealousy, my dear Sophia. It is not worthy of you. Besides, Mary is not to be married until her fiancé returns from the Indies in the spring."

Sophia, reflecting upon the part played by chance in this life, reflected that Lieutenant Simpson's ship might well sink before his wedding; then, suitably shocked by her own reflection, took to heart her mother's admonitions on jealousy, and tried to accommodate herself resignedly to the domestic confines of the Rectory.

It was well at that juncture that she did so. Mrs Lockley, in claiming, and delighting in, Sophia's company, did not explain that she had great need of it. An illness that had affected her intermittently for some time was now gaining upon her and assuming, she knew, fatal proportions. Mary's wedding was the last family occasion that she attended, and for that she required all Sophia's support. Soon afterwards she sank into a rapid decline, to the dismay and grief of her unsuspecting husband. Only to Sophia had she confessed her state, and that not until it was beyond the powers of the doctors to save her.

Two

The death of Mrs Lockley was a severe affliction to all at the Rectory, who had much loved and needed her. To Sophia, before she had begun to recover from her own sadness at her mother's loss, came the unconsoling recognition that henceforward the running of the household would devolve upon herself. To Mr Lockley, there could be no question of anything else; Sophia's duty was to take her mother's place. Sophia, brought up as she had been to value the stern principles of her father and the gentler, but equally just, principles of her mother, could not question either where her duty lay. But she contemplated her responsibilities with misgivings, and her own future with desolation. It would have helped her, had her father showed her any gratitude or given her any encouragement; but Mr Lockley's manners did not at any time admit display of affection, and his bereavement had the effect on him of intensifying his reclusiveness. He shut himself in his study, impatient of interruption, and impatient of any failure of the domestic routine. As soon as Sophia had to submit the household account-books to him, he reproved her because the expenditure was higher than it had been under his wife's management, but had no advice to give on how this

might be remedied. He had left all such matters to Mrs
Lockley and had no idea of the devices she had used to keep
within her housekeeping allowance. Too late, Sophia
wished she had paid more attention to her mother's
concerns instead of dilating always upon her own. She had
very little idea, left to herself, of household governance, and
she was very much left to herself, in this matter as in
everything. Her only counsellor was the girls' old nurse,
Sally, who had been with the family since the first baby was
born, and had not been young then; she was now elderly,
becoming forgetful. She too had left all practical affairs to
Mrs Lockley.

The prospect before Sophia appeared, with good reason,
bleak. The falling leaves of that autumn revealed to her only
the emptiness of the neighbourhood. The Rectory itself was
a pleasant enough house, having been rebuilt in modern
times by a wealthier incumbent at some distance from the
church, on an eminence looking down the valley towards
the village, but with its outlook now blocked by thickets of
untended woodland. The village was inconsiderable, and
the nearest town, Bardton, more than five miles away.
Beyond the Rectory, the road up the valley passed only one
house of respectable size, and a couple of cottages, before
climbing to the open moorland. The one house was
tenanted by a valetudinarian retired corn-merchant, his
solicitous wife and an orphaned granddaughter. The whole
estate was nowadays neglected; its owner had formerly
come up from London for the shooting season, but was now
an old man who, according to report, spent his time at
cards. It may be that he gambled away his money. At any
rate, there seemed none to spare for the upkeep of the manor-
house, whose stable roofs had collapsed altogether last
winter and whose avenue was blocked by fallen elms. The
agent who was supposed to deal with the property was an

elderly man too, perpetually harassed and inevitably ineffectual. He, a Mr Mallet, was one of the few neighbours who occasionally dined at the Rectory. In all the countryside there seemed to be no one at all of Sophia's age. She could scarcely believe now that, so few years ago, the Rectory had been such a crowded bustle of family life, resounding (at least when Mr Lockley was not in the house) to the quarrels and laughter of children. Her circle was as depleted at home as abroad.

Sophia still had her two youngest sisters with her, and it was here that she felt her responsibility to lie the heaviest. With them, she could never replace their mother, but they had no one else to turn to. She felt some anxiety about each: Claudia was a handsome, energetic girl but with a defiant spirit; she was a favourite of old Sally, who had tended to spoil her. Lucinda was quieter, a retiring and intelligent girl; she had made a friend of the granddaughter of the old couple in the nearby house, with whom she studied French and practised duets on the pianoforte; but Lucinda, of all the robust Lockleys, was the delicate one; Sophia was now afraid that an illness such as her mother's was possible in the family.

Still under the heaviness of her mother's death, Sophia had an earnest and humble desire to fulfil as well as she could her duty to each member of the household. She would keep within her budget by stringent means, curb her irritation with Sally, provide her father with clean linen and faithful assistance in parish affairs, gently guide Claudia towards a more docile attitude, cherish Lucinda through the chills of winter, write often to her other sisters, with cheerful accounts of home; for her mother's sake she would submerge herself.

That was the resolve of her immediate appraisal. She shut away all thought of the future, in which chance, if it were to play a part, must needs play a miraculous one. Wryly, she permitted herself the supposition: "The best I can hope for, in these circumstances, is that I shall be able to find husbands for both Claudia and Lucinda." With chance favouring, as usual, everyone but herself, she did not doubt that she would be able to do so.

Three

That autumn and winter passed wretchedly for everyone in the Rectory. Close as the little group was in sympathy, the disparity of age and temperament prevented real understanding. Mr Lockley's unhappiness worked inward upon himself, and his nerves suffered from Sophia's anxious attentions, Claudia's boisterousness and Lucinda's shy silence; but as he felt it would be undignified, and self-indulgent, to display his preferences to his dear daughters, he merely presented to them a more aloof and forbidding front; whereupon Sophia became more anxious, Lucinda more timid, and Claudia seemed unable to enter or leave a room without slamming the door.

They had hoped for visitors at Christmas, but it happened that, that year, Margaret the eldest daughter was obliged to entertain a number of the Merton relations, Anne was about to have a child, and Mary was with her naval husband in Gibraltar. Priscilla and her husband travelled north to celebrate the holidays at the Rectory, but celebration was hardly achieved and in the New Year a heavy snowfall closed most of the roads for several weeks. By the time a slow thaw began to promise spring, Lucinda had a persistent cough. Sophia thought her thin and pale;

and, think little as she might of herself, she observed in her glass that her own complexion had lost its brilliance. Other preoccupations still prevented her from worrying over this: household mishaps – such as smoking chimneys, frozen water-butts and pilfering housemaids – multiplied as Sophia was sure they never had done in her mother's time.

With the coming of spring came a measure of relief. Lucinda's health improved; Margaret wrote to suggest that Claudia make a long visit to Suffolk. Sophia thought this an excellect idea and was disappointed that her father opposed it.

"She is too young and unrestrained in her manners to go into society," Mr Lockley pronounced. "Besides which, I should prefer her to remain at home until the family is out of mourning."

Claudia received her father's edict with indignation. "How can it be called going into society, simply to visit one's own sister?" she demanded of Sophia. "As for being young – I am almost sixteen!"

"Perhaps it is your manners that cause father to overlook that."

"And how am I to improve my manners, might I ask, hidden away here, where we see no one –"

"We shall have more company presently, I expect, as summer comes –"

"To be sure, Mr Williams and his mother will come to dinner. And Emily Gray and her grandmother will drink tea. Such excitements should be enough for anyone of my supposed age."

"Dear Claudia, be patient. Remember how pleased Lucinda and I are to have you at home, if our society is as limited as you say."

"I am sure you do nothing but bite my head off. You would have been gladder to be rid of me."

Sophia felt this reproach unjustified, but said only: "I am sorry if I appear to check you too much. But you know how noise in the house distracts our father, and that Lucinda is not as energetic as yourself, and needs rest."

Claudia sighed heavily, and went off banging the door to practise with as vigorous a touch on the old schoolroom pianoforte. Sophia from that time tried to soften her own manner towards her intractable sister, and after a while was rewarded; Claudia quite suddenly became more serene and contented and ceased to lament her relegation to the surroundings of home. Sophia, much relieved, ascribed the improvement to the fine weather, during which Claudia and Lucinda took long walks together about the country, to the benefit of Lucinda's health, as well as of Claudia's temper.

The mid-summer passed peacefully, and Sophia was finding life dull rather than harassing when, accidentally, she was undeceived as to the source of Claudia's new happiness. The accident came about through Lucinda who one day returned home to display her basket half filled with purple bilberries, of which she said she had found a thick patch at the moor's edge. Sophia, pleased to have any free supplement to the family menu, remarked that it must have taken the girls a long time to gather so many of the little berries.

"But I picked them all myself," Lucinda assured her. "It was while Claudia was ..." she checked herself, in confusion, and added: "... a little way away."

"I do wish, Lucinda, that you and Claudia would not separate when you are out of doors. What if one of you should fall, or lose your way, in those lonely places?" Then she observed Lucinda's blush, and asked: "Why was Claudia not with you?"

Lucinda's confusion deepened with her colour. She could

only murmur: "Claudia made me promise. I can say nothing. Please do not ask me."

Lucinda was gentle, but scrupulous; Sophia would not pain her by insistence. When she applied to Claudia, insistence gained nothing. By now alarmed – Claudia's laughing denials themselves provoked suspicion – Sophia appealed to old Sally, whose loyalty overcame her promises to Claudia. She told Sophia that she had sworn not to tell, but that Claudia had formed an association with a certain Joseph Hodgson, the young son of a farming family a couple of miles away across the moor. Sally made little of it; the Hodgsons were 'decent enough folk' and Miss Claudia was a good girl and deserved a little harmless pleasure, and anyhow, who was to care? asked Sally; adding that the Rectory manservant had heard in Bardton market that young Joseph Hodgson had spent a deal of time lately riding the length of his father's land in search of lost sheep.

This joke, if such it was, was lost upon Sophia. Earnestly she persuaded Sally of the indecorum, to say the least, of Claudia's conduct. Her persuasions on Lucinda and Claudia were heartfelt and, she thought, effective, although Claudia affected to shrug off the topic. Keeping a strict watch on her sister, Sophia hoped that the liaison had been terminated and that she need not tell her father of it.

As the year mellowed, and the girls wanted to range the countryside for blackberries and nuts, Sophia accompanied them. No sign of Joseph Hodgson was seen. Catastrophe occurred, however, one day when Mr Lockley, returning earlier than he had expected from some business in Bardton, decided to visit a sick parishioner in a cottage beyond the village. Thither Claudia had been sent by Sally, to deliver some broth; and Mr Lockley approaching the cottage, perceived his daughter and a strange young man strolling hand in hand beneath the beeches of its lonely lane.

His shock and anger were extreme. He blamed Sophia, especially when she confessed that she had known previously of Claudia's imprudence. Sophia, admitting the justice of her father's censure, blamed Sally, who was still impenitent: Yes, she had been hearing from the gardener's wife, whose cousin was dairy-maid at the Hodgsons', of the movements of young Joseph, and had continued to guide Claudia's accordingly, and to engineer meetings. "You are too severe on her, Miss Sophia, "Sally said. "Nowadays you are getting too severe altogether and I'm sorry to say it."

Sophia's severity was at this point less than her father's. Ignoring Claudia's protests that she and Joseph loved each other and intended to marry, Mr Lockley forthwith packed her off to Suffolk to the care of her eldest sister, setting no term to the visit. From Suffolk, Margaret presently wrote to Sophia:

"... Claudia is being very trying. She has quite set her heart on marrying this yokel, she maintains, and refuses to join in any of the entertainments I offer her. I do feel you should have been firmer with her, and I do not understand how you allowed this situation to come about ..."

The Rectory was quiet indeed without Claudia, and during the winter another loss befell the neighbourhood: Mr Gray, the infirm and retired tenant of the house nearest to the Rectory, died. Few had known more of him than his wife's reports on his health, according to which it was astonishing that he had so long survived. Few would miss him, but the one most affected by this event was Lucinda, who as a result of it lost her friend Emily. Mrs Gray removed to the south of England to be nearer to her own relatives and took her granddaughter with her. The house, which was called Ladysmead, stood empty and was likely to fall into the same dilapidation as the manor-house and most of the cottages of the estate.

The prospect from the Rectory was thus rendered more cheerless than ever. Meanwhile, however, Claudia, relieved of it, and stimulated in spite of herself by new scenes and company, gradually abandoned her obstinacy in favour of more amiable tactics and began to appeal for Margaret's sympathy in her plight, enrolling it as effectively as she had that of Sally and Lucinda. Margaret wrote to Sophia that Claudia was truly unhappy, and sincerly devoted to the farmer's boy; could he really be as impossible as one had imagined? What did Sophia know of the family, and how obdurate was Mr Lockley likely to be? Claudia had shown Margaret a part of a letter from the young man, and he was at least literate. Would Sophia perhaps suggest an interview between her father and Joseph Hodgson's?

This *volte-face* surprised and dismayed Sophia. If Margaret had been permitting a correspondence between Claudia and her swain, she had assumed an initiative that she must maintain; Sophia dare not plead Claudia's cause with her father. Then, wrote Margaret in return, she and her husband would travel north as soon as the weather was milder, and bring Claudia home and arrange everything satisfactorily.

It must be said at once that Claudia's constancy was rewarded, if not without difficulties, in whose solving Sophia felt she herself played little part. Indeed, everyone seemed to feel she had been in the wrong side of every phase of the affair. Privately she was still not sure that Claudia would be really happy in the life of a moorland farm, but this opinion she kept to herself. "Who," she asked herself, "would in any case heed my opinion?"

It was a great pleasure to her in the first instance to have a visit from Margaret, on whatever pretext. Margaret had always been the sister closest to her in age and tastes and they had been so long separated. They took time amid the negotiations of Claudia's future to have many confidential conversations about their own.

"But you must not feel obliged to settle yourself here for ever," Margaret told Sophia. "You are looking tired, and you frown too much. I know it has been a difficult time for you, but you will regain your looks as soon as Claudia is settled and the worry is over. Soon, Lucinda will be old enough to look after the household and Father, and she will do very well – She is a mousy little thing and not fond of society – And then you must come down to me, and we shall find you a husband and settle you nearby, and we shall see a good deal of each other."

Sophia smiled but shook her head, sceptical of this daydream. Events had relieved her of the task of finding a husband for Claudia, but she could not absolve herself of the task in Lucinda's case, or bequeath to Lucinda the duties that she herself found so onerous. The planning of the wedding, for mid-summer, presented difficulties enough to absorb her. It was not a splendid occasion; but all was done as lavishly as Sophia thought her father would allow, and the mingling of Lockley and Hodgson guests was achieved without embarrassment on either side. The bride-groom Sophia had found on making his acquaintance to be a pleasant ruddy-faced young man, no more awkward than might be expected of someone not yet twenty years old and more accustomed to the company of sheep than to that of a variety of humankind. Evidently he was devoted to Claudia, and his attachment had, like hers, withstood their winter's separation. Mr Williams the curate performed the wedding ceremony, and Mr Lockley gave away his sixth daughter with as little apparent regret as he had permitted himself to show on bestowing any of the others. Claudia was borne off radiant among her bucolic henceforward connections, and was by her messages soon happily established at Ashcross farm. It was because she wished to share this happiness, and not because she in any way regretted her change of scene, that she urgently asked Lucinda to come and visit 'for as long as she liked.' Sophia encouraged Lucinda to go. She was afraid Lucinda, missing both Claudia and Emily Gray, would be lonely, and the upland air would be good for her health besides.

So a farm cart collected Lucinda and took her away up the valley, its driver, an elder brother of Joseph Hodgson's, remarking that he could not promise to bring her back again 'till after the harvest.' Sophia was left with her father, taciturn as ever, and Sally, whose treachery she still could not fully forgive; the more so as Sally took all the credit for Claudia's marriage upon herself, and pointed out to Sophia more than once that everything turned out for the best in the end and love would be sure to find a way. Sophia accepted these optimistic sentiments in silence, lest she be tempted to disagree.

Four

It was growing dusk, and smoke was ascending from the cottage chimneys to mingle with a slight mist among the trees of the valley, when the cart from Ashcross Farm delivered Lucinda Lockley home after her visit to her sister Claudia. Autumn already chilled the air and Mrs Hodgson had wrapped Lucinda in extra shawls for her journey. In the cart Lucinda felt warmer than she had, however, at any time during her weeks at Ashcross. There, the doors of the farmhouse were always open with someone hurrying in and out, and for the most of the day one was obliged to be out too, carrying pails of poultry food or milk, or searching the damp hedgerows for eggs. The late summer had been poor, making the hay harvest later, pressing upon the reaping of the scanty crop of oats that the wet season had yielded. It had been a busy time for the Hodgsons and the help given by Claudia and Lucinda had been useful. Claudia was entirely in her element and considered she was giving her sister the most delightful privilege in the world by allowing her to join in the farm's activities. Lucinda had tried to show her gratitude, but even in the jolting of the cart she felt that the headache brought on by the incessant noise of the farm was gradually easing.

Mr Hodgson had three sons who worked on the farm with him, all three of them now married, and the elder two already with children. Also in the house lived a sister of Mrs Hodgson's, a bachelor uncle of Mr Hodgson's, the cousin of the Rectory gardener's wife, who was dairymaid, and several other maids; all the field workers came crowding in daily for breakfast and dinner, unless they were in the further fields, when dinner had to be carried out to them. Everything was done in a bustle; Lucinda's head rang to the hallooing of men's voices, the shrieks of children's, the clack of pattens on the flags of dairy and kitchen, the clang of pans on the stove, the clash of pails, the crowing of the rooster that frightened her before each daybreak. She had never before been in such proximity to cows or pigs and was nervous of them. Claudia, whirling about with rosy face and bare arms, laughed at her fears. There was in the house no sign of a book; conversation was confined to farm affairs or, when the women were at work together, local gossip. On Sundays, the family attended the church in the valley adjacent to Mr Lockley's, where his curate Mr Williams officiated, since this was nearer to Ashcross. So Lucinda, as the road drew down towards her home, was looking forward with some relief to her return, after what seemed long absence.

She had not found life at the Rectory dull, because she preferred quiet pursuits and was sensitive to the beauties of nature, when their impact was not so violent as she had felt them at Ashcross. Lonely she had perhaps been, since the loss of her mother and the varying preoccupations of Sophia and Claudia, and, latterly, the departure of Emily Gray, had deprived her of anyone's special attention; but Lucinda felt herself unworthy of anyone's special attention. She resolved to make the most of the peacefulness of the Rectory, to help Sophia with her work, to try hard to think

of things to say to her father, so that her timidity should not
make him suppose her ungrateful. She was now fifteen, but
had no ambition to venture into the wider world. "I will be
content," was her resolution, as the cart passed the first of
the cottages, from whose window candlelight glinted.
Drawing her shawl closer, she remembered with a pang
that she would shortly pass the gates of Ladysmead and
have to see the house dark and empty. "I will not look at
it," Lucinda vowed to herself. "And the next thing I know,
I shall be at the Rectory gate." But in spite of herself she
did glance aside, and was astonished to see lights in the
drawingroom window and a thread of smoke rising from
the chimney against the darkening sky. Immediately she
thought: "Emily is back!" – but then realised how unlikely
that must be. Undeniably, though, Ladysmead was
occupied. Far from not looking at it, Lucinda craned over
the cart side to gaze at the house. Even in the dusk, she
observed that the gravel sweep, overgrown with weeds
when she left home, was now raked and tidy, and she
believed that some of the shrubs had been cut back. If there
were a new tenant, he had already tended the place more
than even the Grays had. Even the house gleamed whiter
than she remembered through the twilight. It was a well-
proportioned modern house, of about the same age as the
Rectory and probably built at the same stage of the estate's
prosperity. Lucinda, playing there with Emily since she
was five years old, was well acquainted with it and its
garden, and her curiosity to know what was being done
there was greater at first than any curiosity to know who
was doing it.

She was being driven home by her brother-in-law's uncle
Samuel, who wished to go on to Bardton tonight in order to
be early at tomorrow's market. He placed Lucinda's boxes
on the Rectory doorstep and bade her farewell with little

ceremony. Sophia herself came to the door at the sounds of
arrival, and Lucinda's immediate question was:

"Has someone come to live at Ladysmead?"

Sophia in welcoming her sister almost disregarded the
inquiry. "I am glad to have you back," she cried,
embracing Lucinda. " – Yes, there are new tenants. Come
in to the fire, dear, you must be cold. You must tell me all
about Claudia, and how she does. Are you hungry? I meant
to keep you some veal from dinner, but Hester said it
shrank in the roasting – We dined early, Father is gone out
to Mr Pettigrew's – But I will tell them to make you some
cold mutton, we had some to spare yesterday. Sit down –
Draw that chair nearer. I do not know how it was, about
the veal. It looked a great piece when the butcher brought
it. I daresay that it was, Harry Johnson stayed for his
dinner in the kitchen, and you know how he eats. He has
been here today, felling the old apple-tree by the stable
gate."

"The old apple tree? Oh, but I loved it," exclaimed
Lucinda, disencumbering herself of Mrs Hodgson's shawls
and taking the chair Sophia drew to the hearth for her. "I
see it from the window of my bedroom. It was a beautiful
tree."

"Yes, it was a grand old tree, but they said it was
becoming unsafe. A bough fell, in those strong winds a
week or so ago. And now, we shall have firewood for some
time to come, which is a relief to me, because the evenings
are growing chill, and Father has needed the fire in his
study and I was at my wits' end, knowing I ought not to
order more wood till the end of the month. You would like
some mutton, would you not? And there are eggs –"

"No, indeed, I am not hungry. We had dinner at
Ashcross at midday. Do tell me about Ladysmead –"

"I expect they eat well at the farm? They must have all

their own produce to hand, and no thought of expense. You are looking well, Lucie. I think the air has done you good.''

''Yes, I am sure it did. I had plenty of it.''

''We shall have tea presently, then. And Claudia – Is she happy?''

''Yes, very. She works hard about the house and farm –''

''Claudia works hard? That is more than she did here. What has she to do about the farm? She knows nothing of farming.''

''She is learning rapidly. Mrs Hodgson is to teach her how to milk a cow.''

''Well, as long as she is happy,'' remarked Sophia with distaste. ''If Father does not need Brutus one day, and we can have the pony shod, we might both ride up and visit her – if the weather is fit. I think it feels like a frost tonight. I am glad we got the apples picked and stored early, though they were all so small. I do not know how we shall manage through the winter. Would you not like your tea directly? I will call Sally –''

''Please Sophie, I am trying to ask you about the tenants of Ladysmead.''

''Oh, yes. They arrived quite soon after you had gone away. But they are no one of interest. Just two ladies. I am supposed to visit them, but I have been so busy, and I wished to give them a chance to settle.''

''Are they from far away?''

''Yes, I believe so. Sally – who finds out everything – has had it from their servant woman that they are from somewhere in the south. Or the midlands, perhaps she said. Sally thought at first they were a mother and daughter, but now she hears they are an aunt and her niece. Father has called, but he would not, of course, inquire into their concerns. He did tell me, however, that they have both lost their husbands and are seeking a quiet life. Which is certainly what they will find, in this region."

"They are both widows? That is very sad," agreed
Lucinda.

"In truth it is rather sad for us as well. Evidently they do
not intend to add to the gaiety of our society. Well, we need
not bother with them. Tell me about Ashcross. Do they
have much company there?"

Lucinda scarcely knew how to answer that question.
"The company there is constant," she said, smiling. "If you
mean, do they entertain, they do not do so formally – that
is, their friends come and go as they please, but while I was
there no ceremony was made of it."

"Well, I am sorry for Claudia, if these friends are of the
same sort as the Hodgson family. I hope she will not grow
tired of them."

"I think Claudia will grow tired of nothing. She is in
excellent spirits, and in blooming health, plump and pink-
cheeked."

"Then I suppose I should be glad for her," said Sophia
with a small sigh. "And friends coming and going, of
whatever sort, would be preferable to the quietness of this
house nowadays."

Lucinda, after her experiences at Ashcross, could not
wholly agree. She found the quiet of the Rectory restful and
was thankful to be back in her own little bedroom, no
longer shared with Claudia. She slept undisturbed and
woke to a soft misty morning, saddened only by the lack of
the old apple-tree outside her window. At the breakfast-
table her father bade her good-morning with his usual
gravity, and only after some while recollected that she had
been from home, and remarked that she had no doubt
passed her time pleasantly; his tone held so little
interrogation that Lucinda suffered her usual difficulty in
summoning speech to answer him at any length, and her

account of her visit to Ashcross was summarised for him in: "Yes, thank you, Father."

During the ensuing silence, it presently appeared, Mr Lockley had been pursuing his own train of thought rather than waiting for Lucinda to extend her answer. Addressing Sophia he said: "Now that Lucinda is with us again, I feel we should perform our duty to our new neighbours at Ladysmead and invite them to dinner. We should invite Mr Williams and his mother too, since we dined there three weeks ago. Any day of next week will be convenient for me apart from the Monday. I leave you to issue the invitations."

Upon this he quitted the table, barely waiting for Sophia, whose cheek had paled slightly, to say in turn: "Yes, Father." As soon as he had left the room she complained to Lucinda: "I was afraid of this. Now I shall have to call at Ladysmead – Well, you can come with me, Lucie. I had the goose in mind, for Michaelmas, but Hester says it has not fattened and I cannot think what I can supplement it with – And imagine, having two strangers with Mrs Williams – I see nothing to laugh at, Lucie."

"Indeed, I am not laughing," protested Lucinda, smiling nevertheless. "I do admit that it could be a difficult occasion."

"When we dined at the Williams', I declare I came home with the headache. Besides, Mrs Williams had provided an excellent meal, as usual, such as I can never seem to afford."

Mr Williams had been the curate of the parish for the last eight years or so. His widowed mother, who lived with him, was a good-hearted lady and had always been benevolent towards the Lockley girls, who indeed were fond of her for her kindness; but she suffered from a handicap that made her presence in company an infliction: she was very hard of hearing, and apparently unaware of it. Her own voice was exceedingly loud, and her intermittent monologue made a sustained general conversation virtually impossible. Sophia as well as Lucinda had found this sometimes a cause of mirth; poor Mrs Williams's deafness was a family joke of long standing among all the sisters; but Lucinda agreed with Sophia that it could prove an embarrassment in entertaining strangers.

"Perhaps," she said, "if these ladies prefer a quiet life, they will not accept dinner invitations."

"That is more than I dare hope for, especially when the dinner I shall offer will inevitably be of an inferior nature."

"Dear Sophie, please do not be such a pessimist. I am sure you never used to be. Let us promise ourselves that the dinner will be a success, and so it will. And for all we know, the Ladies of Ladysmead may be delightful company; after all, we have not yet met them."

"You are right," conceded Sophia after a moment's recollection. "I am apt to form gloomy expectations of things nowadays; I will try to be less self-discouraging. You are a comfort, Lucie; I am so glad you are back. As for the ladies of Ladysmead – we shall see."

About the ladies in question, Sophia had not been entirely candid with her sister. She had not yet made their acqaintance, but they had been in church, and she had studied them as closely as reverence, and two pews' distance, permitted. What had at once struck her was that these ladies, if desirous of a retired life, were no country mice. Nor, were they widowed, had it been recently, because neither wore mourning. The dress of the elder was neat and fresh; but the younger lady, of about Sophie's age, was strikingly handsome and she was clad in a fashionable elegance quite strange to this parish and to Sophia herself, who recognised its quality by some feminine intuition that effected no improvement of her own spirits. Sophia's interest in the newcomers was shared by most of the other worshippers, but not at all reciprocated; the elder lady kept her attention wholly on the divine service, while the younger's attention seemed wholly abstracted. As all turned to leave the church, the elegant young lady's eyes passed accidentally across Sophia's, but with no pause or spark of interest. On subsequent Sundays her recognition of her surroundings had been as negligible. Once or twice Sophia had seen her riding about the lanes, superbly habited and mounted, but again glancing neither right nor left. It was not surprising that Sophia feared to find this new neighbour unapproachable, in spite of Lucinda's optimism. What dispirited her was to have to confess to herself that she felt something in the nature of shyness, or even the jealousy that her mother had so long ago judged unworthy of her. "Is it possible," Sophia asked herself, "that I am already becoming a countrified old maid, unfit for proper society? I begin to wonder how I should look, and conduct myself, even if I were able to visit Margaret now in Suffolk. – But that is not at present likely to happen, and I must remember that I have my duty to Father, and, Lucinda's affection, and that if I waste time in repining I shall begin to pity myself and be worse for it."

She, like Lucinda, had observed that the new tenants were quick to tidy up the appearance of Ladysmead. According to Harry Johnson, that feller of apple-trees, the tenants had made a great to-do with Mr Mallet about the condition of the place, and Mr Mallet had been writing to old Mr Dalby, the owner, in London, but with no more result than usual. This report made the prospect of calling at Ladysmead no less formidable to Sophia; but as it came about, the necessity of a formal call to deliver Mr Lockley's dinner invitation was avoided.

Two days after Lucinda's return home, she and Sophia
set out to enjoy a walk up the valley, with the object of
taking some linen to one of the cottages, where a new baby
was soon expected. The Rectory's poor-box could provide what Sophia considered only a meagre supply; it
was in this giving of inadequate charity that her generous
nature suffered its deepest frustration. The fine clear day
soon began to restore her mood, and she was talking
cheerfully to Lucinda when at the bend of the lane they
encountered a figure, approaching at a brisk pace and
carrying a basket. It was the elder of the Ladysmead
tenants and, suddenly face to face, they could not have
avoided her had they intended to. They greeted each other
and congratulated themselves agreeably upon the fineness
of the day, and Sophia presented her sister to the lady,
whose name she knew to be Mrs Norris.

Mrs Norris acknowledged Lucinda's curtsey with a nod
and a glance of shrewd appraisal. "There is a likeness
between you," she observed. "How old are you?" And, on
Lucinda's telling her: "You will fill out soon, I expect. At
present, neither of you looks particularly robust." Lucinda
felt too, under that glance, that the fatigue of Ashcross had
left rough traces on her complexion and hands. "You do
well to take exercise, but it does not do to be always
strolling about in the sunshine. I owe my own excellent
health to my energetic nature and to my habit of always
occupying myself with something useful. As you see,"
uncovering her basket, "I have been walking myself, but it
was in order to gather up some of the wild crab-apples that
have fallen from the tree yonder. They will be made into
jelly, and we shall be glad of it in the winter. I am used to a
country life, and know how to make these little economies,
by making use of wild fruit, for instance. I pride myself, in
my small way, on letting nothing go to waste. You might

gather up some crab-apples yourselves and follow my example."

Sophia, who had made crab-apple jelly a week ago, forebore to say so, but instead took this opportunity to extend her father's invitation to dinner at the Rectory on any day except the Monday of next week.

"Please thank Mr Lockley very kindly. I explained to him when he called on us that we do not intend to go much into society here. However, dinner with one's clergyman hardly counts as society, and I am sure it is very civil of him to invite us. My own late dear husband was a clergyman too, so I can sympathise with all the cares of a parish that fall upon him. I must, before I positively accept, consult my niece. She is not much inclined for company nowadays, after the great unhappiness she has had. She needs an amount of seclusion and peace, to mend her spirits. I shall try to persuade her, and then send to tell you if she will come."

Sophia said they would be very pleased to receive both ladies, and hinted that dinner would possibly be on a more modest scale than they were accustomed to.

"Oh, my dear," cried Mrs Norris, "think nothing of that. Who would expect anything else in this neighbourhood, and besides, my niece has dined enough in grand houses to last her for some while. No, it will be quite unnecessary to go to any trouble for us. Just to cross the lane for a little change of scene will surely do Maria good. I shall tell her so."

They prepared to part, Sophia expressing the hope that Mrs Norris and her niece were finding Ladysmead comfortable and would be happy there. This halted Mrs Norris:

"We shall be happy, anywhere where we may be together, and where I can devote myself to Maria, which is

now my chief concern in life. But as for *comfortable* – I have
never known a house in such a shocking state of disrepair. I
will give my oath that the roof leaks into the attics in a
dozen places, half the window-frames are rotting, and now
my cook tells me that as soon as the wind turns north the
kitchen range smokes so that she can hardly go near it. The
agent promises to see to all this, but does nothing, and for
the smoking of the range he is unable to account at all. As
for the state of the gardens –"

Here Lucinda ventured to interrupt. "Excuse me,
ma'am, but I remember that Mrs Gray had that same
trouble in the kitchen, with a north wind, and I believe I
can explain –"

"You are a prodigiously clever girl, if you can explain
what has baffled the experience of my cook and myself, and
even the agent," said Mrs Norris in a discouraging tone.
Sophia felt it just to interpose:

"My sister was on intimate terms with Mrs Gray's
granddaughter, and in the house often. Perhaps she heard
some discussion of the matter?"

"Well, if you did, let us hear the result of it," Mrs Norris
challenged Lucinda, who haltingly began her exposition:

"Mrs Gray thought, do you see, that there had at one
time been another stove in the room that backs on to the
kitchen. The Grays used it as a scullery. There is an old
fireplace there. The Grays blocked it in. But its chimney
shared with the chimney of the kitchen range and, where
they joined, there was an old damper that sometimes fell
loose. Then, Mrs Gray would have George – the boot-boy –
unblock the chimney, and he would reach in, and somehow
replace the damper – I do not quite understand how it was
done –"

"Nor do I quite understand all this about dampers, and

what it has to do with the change of wind," declared Mrs Norris.

"I am repeating only what I håve heard Mrs Grày say," Lucinda maintained, not at all sure that her contribution had been either clear or helpful. But Mrs Norris was not as sceptical as she sounded:

"Well, we shall see whether there is anything in what you say. You had better come with me to the house, directly, and show me where this other chimney is." Upon Sophia's mildly protesting that she and Lucinda had been on an errand up the valley, Mrs Norris said: "Oh, never mind that just now. You can walk on afterwards, or I shall send a servant. Come along, let us see to this business." And she marched them back to the gates of Ladysmead without delay.

So Sophia's call at the house was performed without ceremony, by way of a side-door. Mrs Norris summoned a manservant and led the party to the offices. It was true that, in the scullery Lucinda indicated, a teak board blocked in an old fireplace. The servant removed the table that stood before it and asked:

"Do you want me to try and get the board out, ma'am?"

"Yes, do so, by all means. Be quick. It should be simple enough. I cannot see that it is nailed in place. Come, man, what are you hesitating for?"

The man, doubtfully eyeing the ladies' dresses, suggested that it might be a 'dirty job', but Mrs Norris urged him to perform it. He did so, easily enough, but he had been right: a shower of soot tumbled down as the board was loosened, and rose into the air to descend in a fine film over the whole room and its occupants. The manservant peered into the chimney, then fetched a rod and explored with that, and announced that there was indeed a metal damper rattling free up there, but that he could not reach it; it required someone very much slighter, who could enter the chimney.

Lucinda interposed: "That, I dare say, is why George the boot-boy used to replace the damper."

Sophia gave her a warning look. She feared Lucinda was quite capable of offering to climb into the chimney herself, as the slightest person present, and in her awe of Mrs Norris. Mrs Norris said only:

"I wonder Mrs Gray did not secure the thing permanently, if it was the cause of the trouble. Or that she did not tell the agent to see to it. People are very negligent, and will often put up with inconvenience rather than get to the root of a problem. I believe in being thorough, and am never content to let things remain half-done. I shall send for Mr Mallet about this. Quite possibly," she added to Lucinda, "you were right about the cause of the smoking. It was fortunate that I met you this morning."

Sophia could hardly agree, since the meeting led to the return home of herself and Lucinda sprinkled with soot, their equally sooty linen undelivered. Sally scolded them as if they were children again. There would be all that extra washing, she complained, and why should they trouble themselves about the smoking chimneys of anyone else's house, when the Rectory chimneys smoked as they did? She relented enough to ask Lucinda what she had thought of the ladies, and what the house looked like inside; was it much changed from Mrs Gray's style? Lucinda explained that they had not seen the main rooms, or the younger lady, who had, she thought, been playing the pianoforte in the distance during their visit.

"I daresay she would," Sally said. "She looks a well-born lady and will have all the accomplishments." This remark, Sophia felt, was directed at herself. Since the troubles over Claudia, Sally and Sophia had never regained their earlier good terms. Sophia was even afraid that Sally complained of her to the other servants, setting them against her as they need not have been. She now told Sally that the ladies from Ladysmead might be coming here to dinner next week, but the invitation had not been finally accepted. Sally expressing the wish that folk would make up their minds, made Sophia feel that that complaint too was directed at herself. Her morning had not ended as happily as it had begun, and, perhaps rendered unjust by her depression of the moment, she wondered whether the tenants of Ladysmead were not going to be an unwelcome intrusion into her life, rather than a welcome addition to it.

Five

Mr Lockley, when he heard that his new neighbours would accept his dinner invitation for the Thursday, and established that his curate would also attend, looked forward to the event with no pleasure. This sentiment he would not have thought of sharing with his daughters. Mr Lockley was becoming confirmed in that innocent selfishness of one who makes a virtue of keeping his feelings private. Much that he would have confided to Mrs Lockley, he wished to spare Sophia. Recently, for instance, he had heard from his daughter Mary that her husband, the naval lieutenant, had contracted some debts that he had no means of paying. Her appeal to her father had not been in vain, but Mr Lockley, worried about the steadiness of Lieutenant Simpson, did not want Sophia to be worried on Mary's account, so informed her only that an additional demand on his income had made additional domestic economies necessary. His gravity of manner made Sophia fear that, if too much were provided for the dinner-table, he might order its removal. She consulted Lucinda, who seeing her sister anxious, could offer no consolation beyond:

"I really do not suppose Father will notice what we are eating, once the guests are here. And it might have been worse: he might have invited Mr and Mrs Mallet as well."

"Oh, pray do not mention that when he is near – He may yet wish to!"

But they were spared the Mallets. On the Thursday, Mr Williams and his mother arrived punctually, and Mrs Williams preceded her son into the Rectory drawingroom with a beaming countenance. She, of all the company, was probably the only member disposed truly to enjoy this evening's festivity. She was a rotund, tidy little woman in her mid-fifties, always ready to make the best of her circumstances, which was as well, because her life had not been altogether fortunate. She came of good, but not wealthy, connections and had married a gentleman similarly placed, but of delicate health. When he died, Mrs Williams had had little help with the upbringing and education of her only child, Charles. It was to her credit that he had been able to take orders, and he was grateful for all the sacrifices she had cheerfully made to this end. He had little hope of advancement beyond his present curacy, but Mrs Williams was content to have him as well established as he was, and to care for him was her great satisfaction.

She was, naturally, quite aware of her deafness, and was afraid only of causing embarrassment to others, by requiring them to shout at her and repeat their remarks. Hence she had developed her style of conversation, which involved imagining questions and answering them for herself. She began as soon as she entered the room:

"My dear Mr Lockley, how are you? Well, I am sure, though you will be tired after riding to Bardton and back today – Charles told me you had to go in. The roads were dreadfully muddy, did you not find? But of course, after that rain, what else could one expect? Sophia, how pretty your gown is – You did not make it yourself, I know; Anne was always the needlewoman of the family. How is she? And the children? Very well, I hope. Dear Lucinda, are you home again now? Did you enjoy your visit to Claudia's? Yes, you were glad to be with her, and she will soon want you with her again, because it is a lonely life, on a farm so far from everywhere, is it not? Does she dread the winter, in such a bleak place as Ashcross? I would myself. Is she happy, however? She must be happy, among the Hodgsons. I have always found them good-hearted, well-meaning people. The youngest boy, her husband – Joshua is his name, is it not? Yes, Joshua – was quite a favourite of mine when he was a little boy and used to ride down to school on his pony. One day I caught him gathering windfall apples from beside our orchard, and I was about to speak to him sharply, but then I saw he was splitting the apples for his pony –"

All this was delivered in a voice that made the walls of the room echo, and in the time that it took for Mrs Williams to seat herself in the chair offered by Mr Lockley. Nor, till the tale of little Joseph Hodgson's pony was ended, could any other voice be heard. When the story was done, Mrs Williams felt her duty to be done for a while also, and sat smiling attentively at the others, whose conversation was to her a faint murmur, as if she had her ear to a beehive. Her son Charles took a chair beside hers, so that he might inform her of anything significant that was said. From long practice, he had hit on the pitch and placing of his voice that his mother could most easily catch.

Charles Williams was now thirty-three years old, a tall, not ill-favoured man with a quiet manner. He turned to Lucinda, who sat at his other side, and said:

"I hope you did indeed enjoy your visit to Ashcross? I was glad to see you among them in church."

"I was very glad to see you too," Lucinda told him,

sincerely. Among all those strangers, Charles Williams's face had been of a comforting familiarity. "And, Mr Williams, I did so much admire your sermon about the harvest – about the little seeds that had fallen into the ground and died, that all this plenty might come. It was a valuable lesson in humility."

Charles Williams's smile held a hint of friendly mockery. "It is gratifying to know that my sermon's are listened to. But you, I am sure, need no lessons in humility."

Lucinda disclaimed, blushing; they went on to discuss Ashcross and its residents, of whom Charles Williams had no low opinion. He was able to draw Lucinda out into conversation; she could not be shy with him. But as they talked, although he could not allow himself to show it, Charles's attention was divided, half of it attracted to the exchange between Mr Lockley and Sophia, about the state of the fire, and whether more logs should be brought in to last out the evening.

It was suspected by no one that Charles Williams felt a very deep affection for Sophia Lockley. Since he had first known the family, eight years ago when all were still at home, he had singled out Sophia as his ideal of feminine beauty and charm. He had had no thought of telling her so, or of in any way hoping to attract her affections towards himself. He had thought himself too sober and dull for her; he did not see that he could marry at all, while his mother occupied the chief place in his household and had such a claim on his attention; and, since the death of Mrs Lockley, he had come to understand from observing her that Sophia was not happy in the duties of a clerical home; he could not expect her to exchange one for another. It grieved him to see her struggling under her responsibilities, and to see the little frown that her sister Margaret had commented on appearing more frequently on her brow. He felt helpless to relieve her and was anxious not to be too obtrusive in giving what friendship he could, lest she divine his attachment.

Mrs Williams now, after watching Mr Lockley's inspection of the log basket, re-entered the party. "Are those apple logs?" she trumpeted. "Yes, nothing but apple wood gives such a good flame. Do you burn much wood? We use a good deal, too. I like to see a cheerful fire. But have you not found the nights wild, this autumn? No, we have had scarcely any frost yet. Shall we have snow before Christmas? Yes, I expect so. When there has been a wet summer –"

Her son here gently touched her sleeve and indicated that the door of the room was opening for the other guests to be announced. Mrs Williams turned, all smiling interest, as the servant ushered in: 'Mrs Norris and Mrs Rushton.'

Mrs Rushton's demenour this evening was very much as Sophia had observed it in church; she displayed no curiosity at all towards her surroundings, apart from one quick stare of amazement at Mrs Williams when that lady first gave utterance. Mrs Norris, except when eclipsed by those same utterances, was loquacious, as if to cover her niece's silence. When they moved into the dining-room she at once praised it, and the dinner that was being set before them.

"This room has good proportions," she told Mr Lockley, "and it is not too crowded with furniture. I declare I hate to see a room with too large a table, or any other form of ostentation. Miss Lockley," turning to Sophia, "there was no need at all for you to apologise for the modest scale of your hospitality. It is entirely adequate, and suitable to the standard one expects to find in country such as this. Do you not agree, my dear Maria, that a simple dinner, excellently served, is as good in its way as the most elaborate banquets you have attended in the circles you have been used to move in? I am sure you are grateful that Miss Lockley has gone to no excessive trouble for our sake."

Sophia looked to Mrs Rushton, wondering how she would answer that remark, which Sophia herself would have found virtually unanswerable; Mrs Rushton took the course of making no answer at all. Mrs Norris continued:

"I am of a prudent, not to say frugal, nature myself, and pride myself on being able to make many useful little economies in the running of a household. My late dear husband held a good living, but there were so many demands upon him, in the way of hospitality and charity, that it often needed my wisdom to keep us out of difficulties. I shall hope to be as useful to my niece, in guarding her from extravagance, as her circumstances have been reduced much lately." To Mrs Williams she added confidentially lowering her voice: "My niece has been most cruelly used by her family. I alone have supported her. But I prefer not to speak of her private affairs, of course."

Mrs Williams, with no idea of what Mrs Norris's words had been, saw that they had been accompanied by a solemn nod, so nodded solemnly in return, a response quite satisfying to Mrs Norris. Mrs Rushton varied her expression so far as to direct an irritated glance towards her aunt, but she did not speak. Charles Williams sustained the talk, by beginning to speak of local topics to Mr Lockley, who, as Lucinda had foreseen, ate his dinner with his normal grave indifference. All passed well; only when they returned to the drawingroon was there some little hesitation over how the remainder of the evening was to be passed.

"Have you no pianoforte?" asked Mrs Norris glancing about her. "I am sure Maria would have been delighted to play for you. She is a gifted musician, in addition to her other talents."

Sophia had to explain that the Rectory pianoforte, after being practised upon by seven little girls in turn, had been retired with its honourable scars to the old schoolroom.

"You must miss a good instrument, if you are musical yourself. We have a very fine one at Ladysmead. It gives you hours of pleasure, does it not, Maria? Only today," Mrs Norris went on, "she was looking out a book of duet pieces, that she used to play with her sister, and regretting that my fingers are much too stiffened with useful tasks to enable me to play the second part for her. Perhaps, Miss Lockley, you would be pleased to have the opportunity of playing with her."

Sophia had to regret that she had not been able to keep up with her music of late. "My sister is more proficient than I," she admitted, rather to the alarm of Lucinda, especially as Mrs Norris at once said:

"Then Miss Lucinda, you must come and try some of the simpler pieces. Maria will not be critical, and will be obliged to you."

Lucinda could only say that she would be happy. She was relieved that Mrs Norris said no more of music, but returned her attention to the rest of the gathering and suggested a table of whist. For this, the two gentlemen made up the four with Mrs Norris and Sophia. Meanwhile, Lucinda brought the family album of pressed flowers to show to Mrs Williams, and Mrs Rushton sat like a graceful statue except that her eyes moved several times to the clock in the corner. Before the store of apple logs was burned away, the company had departed with thanks, variously expressed, for a very pleasant evening.

"So, you see," said Lucinda to her sister, "it was all a success, and you need not have worried."

"No, I suppose everyone was satisfied, or prepared to say so."

"What do you think of Mrs Rushton?"

"There is nothing to think; I believe she did not speak to me – if to anyone – during the whole time."

"She is the most elegant person I have ever seen. Do you not think she is beautiful? Did you hear what Mrs Norris was saying: that her family had been cruel to her? I wonder how, and why, that was."

Sophia observed: "I feel it is unlikely that we shall ever find that out."

"I am not being inquisitive. – Well, yes, I am, a little. Do you not find her situation mysterious, Sophie? Or interesting?"

Sophia reflected, and said: "No; on the whole, I do not." Mrs Rushton's conspicuous lack of interest in Sophia could not but strike some echo of a negative response.

Six

The rain, that had begun on the day before the dinner at the Rectory, continued without remission for a week. "I am so sorry, my dear," said Mrs Norris to her niece, who was pacing the drawingroom of Ladysmead, "that you have been prevented for so many days from riding."

"I am pretty sorry for myself upon more causes than that," replied Maria, swinging round to pace back. "I cannot find life tolerable at all."

"I sympathise with you, indeed I do, but you must not allow yourself to be despondent. You know that there is nothing in the world I would not do to make you happy."

"So you often say," remarked Maria in a tone of no gratitude.

Mrs Norris had no children of her own and, living close by her sister's family, had made a favourite of Maria since the latter's infancy and could admit no fault in her at all. That Maria had let imprudence lead to misconduct, of a sort that now excluded her from society, had increased her aunt's partisanship; Maria was more than ever, to Mrs Norris, an angel. In this solitude to which they were committed, she was inclined to indulge all Maria's whims and to offer her whatever she could in the way of pleasure;

she had no thought of trying to engage her niece in any useful or improving occupation. Consequently, Maria's boredom was likely to be the greater, and her irritation with Mrs Norris to increase.

"I do wish we could find company for you, of a congenial sort. I wish Miss Lockley were more amiable towards you."

"I should be hard put to it indeed, to accept the amiability of a clergyman's old-maid daughter."

"Then, should we not have the younger one here, to play duets with you? You know how you used to enjoy duets. I am sure she would not presume upon the invitation. I thought at first she might be the sort of girl who put herself forward, with her pretending to know all about dampers and such matters; but when we were at the house I found her quiet and civil enough. Yes, that is just what I shall do. I shall send a note to the Rectory bidding her come tomorrow."

As Maria did not object, this is what Mrs Norris did. When the note was despatched, she found all the duet books and laid them to hand. "It will be something out of the ordinary for the girl, to hear and to play on such a superior instrument. Of course, should her touch be bad, we shall not let her play it. We cannot have your valuable instrument harmed."

"You forget," Maria said," that it is not in effect mine. I have been lent it, from home, until I can obtain another that suits me as well."

"Oh, my dear, but naturally it is yours. Depend upon it, your father meant you to keep it. He would never put you to the expense of sending it back, let alone for all that distance – Everyone knows that these delicate instruments suffer in the moving. I am quite sure, it was understood, the pianoforte is yours."

"That is not what was said. And my father makes me a

generous enough allowance, without adding to it the gift of
a valuable pianoforte."

"And so might he well make you a handsome allowance
– though, shift as I may, I find it hard to run this house on
it, adding all I can of my own small income – So he might
well make you as large an allowance as he can, considering
his own wealth, and considering the way he has treated you
– In forbidding you your own home, he must expect to set
you up in a fitting way, and I am surprised that you can
utter the word *generous* in connection with him; but then,
you were always of a sweet and forgiving nature. You are
too easy-going; it is fortunate that you have me, to look
after your interests."

Maria had said what she did, purely to tease her aunt;
she had no intention of yielding up the pianoforte, a
superior instrument that had always suited her and that she
had 'borrowed' from her father's house when she married.
As for forgiving her father, she had given him scarcely a
thought, nor had she reflected upon the justness of his
attitude to her. She had been humiliated, but not humbled,
by her ruin and was uncertain as yet how she could face a
life of obscurity; its daily trials and tediums were enough to
distract her from deeper thought.

The next morning was again wet, but brought some
promise of pleasure in the form of a parcel of books that
Mrs Norris had ordered for Maria some weeks ago, but
which had been delayed by some incompetence of the posts.
Among the books was a novel that Maria at once began to
read, and became absorbed in. Mrs Norris, seeing her niece
happily engaged, went upstairs to do some sewing and
became absorbed herself in contriving curtains for the
housemaids' room out of two smaller pairs brought from
her own house. She did not hear the approach of a visitor;
the servant went to announce to Maria that Miss Lucinda

Lockley had arrived, about the music.

"Miss *who* ...?" asked Maria, glancing up annoyed from her book. "– Oh, yes. I forgot. Ask her to wait for a moment – I'm busy just now."

Lucinda, damp from her walk in the rain, sat on a chair in the vestibule. An hour and a half passed. Twice, Mrs Norris came downstairs and looked into the drawingroom, then went up again, satisfied that Maria was still peacefully occupied. Dusk gathered; candles were brought. Maria's pages turned. Mrs Norris left her curtains pinned and came down to sit by the fire with her workbox. In the diningroom a servant-girl, new and clumsy, could be heard laying the table. This girl presently came to ask:

"Beg pardon, ma'am, but am I to set a place for the young lady?"

As Mrs Norris regarded the girl with puzzlement, Maria started up. "Oh – that girl! Good God, I had quite forgotten her. The girl from the Rectory, you know, Aunt – What is her name? Call her in," she commanded the servant. Lucinda was brought, to stand shivering slightly before the two ladies. To Mrs Norris's question, she admitted that she had been sitting in the vestibule.

"And she must be cold," said Maria. "It is all my fault. I was reading."

Mrs Norris could not tolerate that anything should be Maria's fault. "Indeed," she said in her sharpest voice, "it was no such thing. It was foolish of Miss Lucinda to hang about, when she knew she was not needed, and she need not expect pity from me, if she is cold. She should either have made her presence known to *me* – Am I not to know who is in and out of this house? – Or she should quietly have gone away again."

Maria, noticing that tears fell from Lucinda's lowered eyes, had an impulse of compassion. "Do not be severe on her," she reproved her aunt. "I dare say she did not know what to do for the best." Laying aside her book and rising, she came to take Lucinda's hand. "Say you forgive me, Miss Lucinda. If you read novels yourself, you will understand how one loses all sense of time."

Maria's smile, and her confidence that she would assuredly be forgiven, charmed Lucinda wholly. She undertook readily to come again tomorrow, and did so, if with trepidation. But she found Mrs Rushton at liberty, and the pianoforte open. Mrs Norris had to satisfy herself that Lucinda's touch would do no harm to the instrument – and indeed, under Mrs Norris's eye, Lucinda was so nervous that she could scarcely touch the keys – but then the duettists were left alone, and were fairly well in accord. Maria was in gracious mood, and amused to remember the country-dance tunes of her childhood; Lucinda in concentrating on the music began to lose her shyness, and to play with more accuracy and spirit.

"You must come again," Maria bade her; and after that, not infrequently a note was sent to the Rectory, requiring Miss Lucinda's attendance at Ladysmead. As the dark days drew in, and the prospect of winter made Maria's outlook even darker, she relieved some of her loneliness by Lucinda's willing and obedient companionship. She could not but be a little flattered to have someone so much flattered by her own attention. To Mrs Norris Maria said: "The girl is no trouble. But as for the rest of this neighbourhood – I might as well be at the North Pole."

North Pole or not, Mrs Norris pointed out, one was not spared all social obligation; they must give a return dinner party, and it was now several weeks since they had been entertained at the Rectory. "We must not appear to be too much above our neighbours, whatever they are, and the Lockleys are a fairly good sort of people. We need not make

a great business of it – they will not expect it, and it might embarrass them if we set a standard too far above theirs. Nor are we obliged, I think, to invite the curate and his bellowing mother. We shall ask Dr Jarrold and his wife."
This doctor, Mrs Norris had called in at various times, when Maria had attacks of headache or listlessness that were at variance with her normally excellent health. Dr Jarrold agreed that Mrs Rushton's general health was unlikely to give cause for alarm, and ascribed her attacks to some passing depression of spirits, which Maria could have diagnosed for herself without medical assistance; Mrs Norris, however, promised that she would never spare effort or expense to ensure that Maria was safeguarded from illness.

Dr Jarrold, then, with his wife, was summoned along with Mr Lockley and his daughters, to dinner at Ladysmead. The doctor was a hearty, ruddy-faced man in middle age, who when he was not riding about the country to visit his far-scattered patients, was riding about it after the fox-hounds. Mrs Jarrold was a frail-looking little lady, exhausted perhaps by bearing the doctor four sons as hearty as himself; some circumstance at any rate had exhausted her conversational ability; she gazed about her to assess the changes made in Ladysmead since the Grays' time, which Mrs Norris was eager to praise to her guests. Mr Lockley was as usual gravely silent, and the doctor applying himself to eating. After dinner, a table for whist was soon made up, with the Jarrolds, Mrs Norris and Mr Lockley, leaving the three young ladies to entertain one another.

Sophia had soon noticed that Lucinda was by now on an accepted footing at Ladysmead, if a subservient one. She was commanded as if habitually to adjust a firescreen, or to bring Mrs Rushton's handkerchief, and showed herself biddable and cheerful. When the three young ladies confronted each other, it was to Mrs Rushton that she looked, as if for a suggestion as to how they might amuse themselves; but Mrs Rushton, though the hostess, said nothing. It was left to Sophia to mention she she would very much like to hear Mrs Rushton perform on the pianoforte, if that would not too much disturb the card-players.

"Oh; very well," Mrs Rushton conceded. "Lucinda, find my Scarlatti sonata – And the Handel suite, you may as well." Off went Lucinda; she might, Sophia felt, still have climbed into a chimney at Ladysmead, for admiration of Mrs Rushton if not for fear of Mrs Norris.

Mrs Rushton played brilliantly, and received Sophia's sincere appreciation not ungracefully; she then asked Lucinda to play some duets with her, for Miss Lockley to hear. But there was still, however it had come about, a certain constraint between these two young women, who, being of the same age, and deprived so much of other society, might have been expected to become friends.

Maria was aware of no special reserve if her attitude to Sophia; she saw her, if at all, merely as one of the dull rustics among whom fate had unkindly thrown her. Sophia, while not permitting herself any active dislike of Maria, found her offhand manners slightly repellent; she could however readily admit Maria's beauty, and admit too that Maria might exert great fascination over someone as young and simple as Lucinda. It was this relationship that began to cause Sophia some anxiety, though she could not have explained why. She was herself relatively simple where the ways of the world were concerned, and could imagine no reason for someone of Mrs Rushton's quality and elegance to select so obscure a style of life. "It is only," she said to herself as she prepared for bed later that night, "that I know nothing of Mrs Rushton; but what can there be, that could harm Lucinda? It is not that I feel anything like a suspicion of Mrs Rushton; I do not know what I could suspect. She is kind, in her fashion, to Lucinda, and is providing her with a change of scene and company that she has so much missed since Emily went away. It is only that Lucinda is so impressionable and easily attached. But so one is, at her age. I am merely imagining that there might be danger for her in this friendship. I am being over-anxious.''

Nevertheless, not long afterwards, she remarked, in spite of herself, one day when Lucinda returned after being a long while at Ladysmead:

"Your music has taken you a very long time today. I believe you must have played all of it a dozen times over.''

"Oh, no; but Mrs Rushton wanted to start some embroidery, and her silks were in such a tangle, I was more than an hour unravelling them.''

"She must be pleased to have you do such a tedious task for her. I expect Mrs Norris is ready to find tasks for you, as well.''

"Oh, yes, there is always some errand or work needed there.''

"Yet you seem happy to be at Ladysmead. I wonder, Lucie, if you are not passing rather too much of your time in helping your new friends?''

"Do you mean,'' asked Lucinda, quickly, "that I am not giving you as much help as I should, at home? I am sorry –''

"No, no. That is not at all what I mean. Perhaps I should be glad to have you with me more often, but not in order to work. It only seems to me, that you are continually in and out of that house.''

"But so I was, when Emily was there. I am sure I spent about half of every day with her, and you never complained then.''

"Nor am I complaining now, my dear. But you must agree, Emily was a very different sort of companion from Mrs Rushton."

"In what way?"

Sophia fancied she heard some obstinacy behind Lucinda's tone. She said: "Emily was of your own age, and of the same interests; and her tastes were less sophisticated –"

"Mrs Rushton and I have many of the same interests. And you know, you told me often enough that Emily and I did not behave well – You said we ought not to climb trees, and that Father would not approve of our reading novels."

"I should be surprised if Mrs Rushton led you into climbing trees," said Sophia smiling. "And you are having valuable practice in your music. In many ways, you will gain benefit from her company. But where novels are concerned, Lucie, I must caution you: What Mrs Rushton considers suitable reading, might not be as innocuous as what Mrs Gray allowed Emily to have. And Father's views on novels, we can be sure, are unchanged."

"You do not read novels yourself," maintained Lucinda. "So I do not know how you can be a judge of them, or of anyone else's tastes."

Sophia said no more. She was afraid that already she might have made it seem she resented her sister's apparent preference of Mrs Rushton's society to her own. Privately, of course, she did, but if she were to show that, it would make matters worse. As it was, Lucinda said to her on the following morning, with a touch of pertness most unusual in her:

"I suppose I may go to Ladysmead now, if there is nothing you require me for?"

"Certainly; you do not need to ask," Sophia said, embracing her. At that, Lucinda laughed and said: "I shall not be late, I promise you."

So Lucinda continued in her attendance and usefulness at Ladysmead, but she grew less ready to describe to Sophia her experiences there. These were not eventful, though occasionally surprising. Lucinda could not have imagined, for instance, that anyone could speak to an older relative as Mrs Rushton sometimes spoke to her aunt. Courtesy had at all times prevailed in the Rectory, between the generations. Lucinda could not accuse her heroine in fact of discourtesy; she could only admire Mrs Rushton's courage in addressing Mrs Norris, of whom Lucinda was still afraid, with such severity. Lucinda was disposed to marvel uncritically in general at Mrs Rushton's moodiness, ascribing it to a deep sensibility. That Mrs Norris should annoy Mrs Rushton, one could not wonder at; if Mrs Norris, chidden by her niece, should turn about and vent her own annoyance on Lucinda, it was no more than Lucinda could bear, when Mrs Rushton would immediately chide her aunt for being cross with 'the poor girl' too. Maria made no attempt to govern her feelings in front of Lucinda, for whose own sensibilities she had no regard. If Mrs Rushton, playing a false note or snapping her embroidery thread, broke into tears of frustration, Lucinda offered a sympathetic silence that concealed her own agitation. For her part, she could not see how Mrs Rushton could describe Ladysmead as 'dull'; it was providing Lucinda with the most interesting winter of her life.

Seven

At Christmas, again, only the loyal Priscilla and her husband made the journey north to visit her family. The other sisters, full as they were of protestations, found it increasingly difficult to leave their homes. Priscilla was still childless, and in any case enjoyed travel, being full of curiosity about the world and its people. She was curious about the tenants of Ladysmead. "... A Mrs Norris, you say? And the other's name is Mrs Rushton?" she asked at the dinner-table on the day of her arrival. "Where do they come from?" And when Sophia had to confess ignorance: "Well, if I were you, I should have found that out by now."

"If you had met the ladies, Pris, I fancy that even you would not."

"Why is that? Are they not friendly?"

Lucinda put in: "They are very friendly to me."

Priscilla's husband, Henry Bolton, suddenly exclaimed: "Rushton? Now there was a great scandal about someone with that name – or a name very like it – in London, not so long ago. Do you remember, Priscilla? it was in the newspapers, and then I heard about it from my cousin who knows some acquaintance of theirs –"

Mr Lockley looked up to say sternly: "If there were any

scandal in London, it would be the last thing I should hope to hear discussed at my table."

"Naturally – I do apologise, sir, and to you, ladies – Besides, I recollect it now," added Henry in a lower voice. "The name in question was not the one you mentioned."

Lucinda, who had been gazing at him alarmed, smiled in thankfulness. Mr Lockley was resuming:

"Now that you have reminded me of our neighbours, it occurs to me, Sophia, that if they have no company for Christmas, it would be our duty to invite them here."

The invitation Sophia duly extended. Rather to her surprise, a note from Mrs Norris replied that she and her niece would be happy to dine at the Rectory on Christmas Day. Sophia was not as dismayed by the prospect as she would have been a few months ago. She was more practised in the affairs of the household as time went on, and she had Priscilla to share the worries with her. "And perhaps," she told Priscilla, "you will be able to inquire of them, to their faces, about all that you wish to discover."

Unfortunately, Priscilla was not able. Only an hour before dinner another note was delivered, regretting that Mrs Rushton was indisposed and that Mrs Norris could not leave her.

"What can be the matter with Mrs Rushton?" asked Lucinda in some terror. "She looked perfectly well in church this morning."

"It may be only some passing ailment," Sophia comforted her, sorry for Lucinda's disappointment as well as for her concern. "Tomorrow, you should go over early, with our inquiries after Mrs Rushton."

This, Lucinda did, to find Mrs Rushton completely restored to health, and apparently having forgotten what had been wrong with her yesterday, as well as that she had missed a dinner-party. It was not explained that what had 'indisposed' Maria was her reluctance to go to the Rectory at all. When Mrs Norris had tried to persuade her, insisting that the invitation had already been accepted, Maria had flown into a rage and accused her aunt of officiousness, heartlessness, stupidity and every other fault that served to feed her fury; and Mrs Norris, who could never resist justifying herself, even when she had offended against her beloved Maria, had entered into a battle against these recriminations that she had better have avoided; it had ended in Maria's locking herself in her bedroom in a tantrum, in the midst of which she wept herself to sleep, so that Mrs Norris, frightened by the sudden silence into supposing that Maria might have done herself some mischief, pounded at the bedroom door till Maria woke in renewed anger, screaming at her aunt that she never wanted to see her again.

In the calm following this storm, Maria kept Lucinda with her for most of the morning, to practise the accompaniments to some new songs, while Mrs Norris sat benignly quiet with her needlework. It was convenient to both ladies at these times to have a third person present, to set them at a more proper distance from each other than they achieved during the scenes that were becoming more frequent, as weather and time kept them shut up together for too long.

Luckily, that winter was mild and at no time was Ladysmead snowed off from the village, indifferent version of civilisation as that afforded. Maria was quite often able to ride about the country, and did so, if only to get away from her aunt for an hour or two. Even this did not much satisfy her. She did not care for solitude, did not think it fitting to enter into conversation with the groom who attended her, and was not used to contemplating the beauties of the landscape. "Those moors go on for ever," she complained to her aunt. "And those lanes in the woods are all the same. I see no one but the occasional curtseying cottager. There is no amusement in circling the same dull routes alone."

"I wish so much, my dear, that I had the leisure to accompany you. But my life has been such as to render me no horsewoman, besides. It is better for me to see to the work, so that you may be free to take exercise –"

"Well," said Maria not listening, "Lucinda can come with me, I suppose."

"But can she ride?"

"I expect so, in a fashion, and if not I shall soon teach her."

Lucinda, when this proposal was put to her, was delighted, but had to confess a difficulty: she had no horse. Mr Lockley's riding-horse had to be always at his disposal; the cob was broken only to harness; and the old pony was still dawdling away his days unshod in the paddock.

"I must say," cried Mrs Norris, seeing Maria disappointed, "that that is a very bad state of affairs. A clergyman should keep up his carriage, and maintain a stable in accordance with his position. He owes it to his position, to live in the style of a gentleman. I know what I am speaking of since my own late husband made a point of having several good horses – eat their heads off as they did; and Mrs Rushton has a brother in orders, who, unfortunate as his life is in many ways – he has married much beneath him – still has to be reckoned a fine horseman."

Maria interrupted her: "My brother's horsemanship is nothing to the point. Lucinda's lack of a horse, is what we are speaking of."

And Lucinda, blushing, dared to say: "I am sure my father keeps as many horses as he can afford, ma'am. He is not a rich man –"

"I dare say he is not – Though he should be able to live as befits a man of standing, and set an example. I do not know what he has to do with his money, with only two daughters at home, and little society. Depend upon it, your sister is not a good enough manager. There are many little savings that can be made, if one has the experience. Dear Mrs Rushton does not know of half the economies I practise for her, to keep up even the simple style of living we have here. Young women need a wiser head to advise them. I should do more, to help your sister, and should be glad to do so – What is my life for, if not to make myself useful to others? – But I am still much occupied in settling matters in this house. I declare, half the gutters still need to be replaced, and Mr Mallet is deaf to my repeated requests. I have my time taken up, with so many difficulties."

Maria, again not listening, had meanwhile conceived an idea: "I could buy a horse for Lucinda, if she can ride. It could be stabled here and kept for her use."

"My dear Maria," cried Mrs Norris in high amazement, "how can you think of putting yourself to such expense?"

"I am sure the expense would not be great, and heaven knows I have little enough here to spend my money on."

"Little enough?" echoed Mrs Norris, even more amazed and indignant. "Dear Maria, you do not for a moment begin to understand these matters. I know you have been used to having as much money as you could wish, and throwing it away without any calculation, but I beg you to recollect that circumstances have changed. It is in your generous nature to be bountiful, but reason must prevail. You must think of yourself. You must take some thought for your future, and, from the pittance you are now allowed, you must try to save, even. Look forward to the time when I shall not be here, to deal with all financial affairs for you, and be prudent."

Perhaps Maria did look forward to such a time, but she was not at the moment unkind enough to say so, being meanwhile planning a method of acquiring a horse. She would tell the groom, she decided, to ask whether there were a horse fair, or anything privately available, in the district. Later in that day she did so, ignoring both her aunt's advice and Lucinda's protests against such a munificent gesture's being made for her.

Lucinda, in referring to her father as not a rich man, was nearer to the truth of the situation than she suspected. Recently, the failure of a hitherto safe concern in which Mr Lockley had made an investment had deprived him of a part of his slender capital. Sophia chose an unlucky time to pass on to him, through a hint of Lucinda's, the suggestion that a riding-horse might be bought for her sister. Neither she nor Lucinda had anticipated the granting of the request, but Mr Lockley's refusal of it was more than final. He added to it:

"I am sorry to have to tell you that I shall have to be more careful of expense in future. I have suffered some losses that may even imperil the very small fortune I can provide for Lucinda if she marries. She would not wish, for the sake of fresh air and exercise now, to deprive herself of what is her due."

The implication that Lucinda, and not Sophia, was expected to marry did nothing to cheer Sophia. Nor did her father's continuing:

"As it happens, I have had a letter recently, from my old friend Mr Shoreham, asking if I might take a pupil he recommends. I do not wish to do so, but feel obliged to resume that practice, in view of my financial need." He sought the letter in his desk, and re-read it as Sophia waited. "I see now, that there are two boys in question. This son of my friend's acquaintance has a schoolfellow who is also in need of tuition and would like to come here with him. It may be that two additional members of the household will not cause much more expense than only one. I look to you to arrange that the expenses are kept minimal."

Sophia, who had by now convinced herself that she knew all about minimal expense and that she had household matters under her control, was thrown into fresh perturbations over the preparation of two bedrooms, the insufficiency of linen for them and the provision for the appetites of two young men. On a fine morning, when Mrs Rushton and Lucinda were at their music, and Mrs Norris had walked over to the Rectory in a rare interval of leisure, to ask for the loan of some preserving-jars, Sophia told her, in the way of conversation, about the expected arrivals.

"My dear Miss Lockley," exclaimed Mrs Norris at once, "I shall be glad to assist you with what advice I can, and be sure I am well acquainted with the ways of young boys, having had a large part in the bringing up of two nephews, the brothers of Mrs Rushton. You will find they eat vast quantities of food, but delicacies are wasted upon them – keep their diet simple, they will be pleased enough. And you should send out their washing, and make them pay for it themselves. You will find them untidy in their habits, so you must be strict with them, and not have your servants put to the trouble of always picking up their books. I hope they will be studious, and not noisy. Unfamiliar as you are with male company, you must not expect young men to be always quiet about the house."

Sophia allowed herself to say: "We did, previously, have a succession of young men in the house, as pupils of my father. Some of them were tiresome, but one of them later married my elder sister." She could not hope, she reflected, that either of these new pupils would be another James Merton.

"Well, but I hope you will make sure that these young men are of excellent character and circumstances, if you have anything of that sort in mind for Lucinda. I am inclined to think she deserves well, better than her lack of fortune might entitle her to. She is an obliging and grateful girl, and her looks are beginning to improve. You must not aim high for her, of course, but she is not to be thrown away."

Sophia accepted this admonition with no reply apart from a faint blush. Rising, she said: "I shall ask Hester about the preserving-jars, if you will be good enough to wait," and hurried from the room.

The two pupils arrived together, towards the end of February. Their names were Robert Davison and Peter Turner. Both were eighteen years old and were intended by their fathers to go up to the university in the following autumn. Both were in need of help with their studies, though these needs had different causes:

Robert Davison had, about a year ago, suffered an accident while skating on a frozen lake. Falling through the ice, he had luckily been rescued, but had contracted a chill that led to a dangerous inflammation of the lungs and kept him for many months an invalid. His parents felt that, although his health was now fully restored, he might be better in a private house than in returning to the rougher life of school.

Peter Turner had not returned to school either after Christmas, but this was because the school had refused to have him, and that was because he was too idle to work, too stupid to see any necessity of work and too uproarious to allow his schoolfellows any peace to pursue their own work.

His parents felt that a secluded clerical household in the far
north might at least spare them from having him at home;
in justice to Mr Lockley's friend Mr Shoreham, who had
recommended both boys, it must be said that Peter
Turner's parents had not been wholly frank about their
reasons for wanting to be rid of him.

Mr Lockley very soon perceived that, while Robert
Davison was an intelligent enough boy, Peter Turner would
not reward the efforts of a teacher; he was dense,
disobliging and dilatory. Mr Lockley set himself however to
do his duty by both pupils. This meant that he took them
into his study for the prescribed hours of tuition, prescribed
their reading and written exercises, then dismissed them
and closed his study door as usual upon the rest of the
house during the time that he was in it. The adjustment of
the domestic background to its newcomers was no concern
of his.

The concern fell, inevitably, upon Sophia. Robert
Davison's manners were gentle and he spent most of his
time in quietly reading. He should have given no trouble,
and certainly intended to give none; but during his months
of illness at home he had been more spoilt by his mother
than he realised. Pleasantly enough, he would mention
that a draught blew under his bedroom door, or that he was
used to a glass of warmed wine before bedtime, or that he
would like the fire built higher, lest he begin to feel chilly.
Sophia, not sure how many of these invalid's habits were
merely habits, had to spend much of her time in attending
to him. Peter Turner, she found worse than any pupil she
could remember or that Mrs Norris could have warned her
of. He threw his clothes all about the floor, tracked mud all
about the house, racketed about the stairs at all hours and
when at rest, sat in the drawingroom with his feet up on a
table, whistling, or enlarging upon his prowess with a gun,

fishing-rod and sailing-boat. Many times during the day
Sophia decided: "I shall complain to my father of him; he is
intolerable." Then she reminded herself that her father
must too be suffering from the noise about the house, and
additionally from having to deal with Peter Turner's
scholarly ineptitude, and she resolved to equal her father in
fortitude.

It did not seem to her that the family finances would be
much improved by the advent of these students. As for the
possibility of either young man's falling in love with
Lucinda, she forgot all about it. In any case, from about
this time, Lucinda was less at home than ever. It happened
that Maria's indirect inquiries after a horse were finally
rewarded: the groom heard that one of Dr Jarrold's sons
had a grey mare that he found 'too tame' for the hunting
field, and that could not be made to leap high hedges. The
mare was brought to Ladysmead, tried out and pronounced
suitable for carrying a lady. Maria purchased it and
commanded Lucinda to prepare for long excursions
henceforth.

Mrs Norris had to accept the deed once done, and even,
since Maria had done it, to put a good face on the
transaction. The mare, if well fed and handled, might be
sold again, perhaps at a profit, if it were no longer needed.
Besides, another perplexity had now arisen, which might
affect the tenants of Ladysmead more than could the
possession of one horse more or less: the news had arrived
of the death of the house's owner, Mr Dalby.

The perplexity came about thus: Mr Dalby's family was
not at all extensive. He himself was over eighty when he
died, relieving himself thereby of his gambling debts, which
were said to be considerable. He had had one younger
brother, who had died some years ago. This brother had
had one son, who had predeceased his father. That son, in

turn, had had one son, Mr Dalby's great-nephew, who now inherited the estate, for what it was worth. But this heir could not be found.

He was known to have been living abroad, but no one could be discovered with whom he had kept in touch. Old Mr Dalby's housekeeper believed the young man had gone to Canada; his manservant thought the West Indies. Mr Mallet reporting all this to Mrs Norris, told her that the lawyers were advertising, and doing all they could to locate her new landlord.

"But he may wish to sell the house over our heads. Or he may wish us to buy it, and who knows what unreasonable price he may ask? It is all most annoying. I dislike uncertainty. And meanwhile, who is to pay for mending the west wall of the orchard? I do not see that we should be put to extra outlay, just because this young man is so tiresome as not to come and look after his own property."

Mr Mallet assured her that the lawyers would continue to handle the affairs of the estate until such time as its new owner assumed his responsibilities. Mrs Norris, unsatisfied, now began to feel that she and Maria were settled very happily at Ladysmead and were quite comfortable in the house, and that it would be a disaster for them if they were to be submitted to the trouble of seeking a new house, and the upheaval and expense of removing.

Eight

The first warm sunshine of spring reconciled Maria, too,
somewhat to her surroundings, and she enjoyed her own
benevolence in providing a mount for her young friend. A
friend, Lucinda was in a small way becoming to Maria,
who was more communicative when out of doors and
relieved of her aunt's proximity, and who had suffered long
enough from having no one to talk to – by which she would
have meant, no one to tell of her own life and affairs, with
all of which Mrs Norris was fully acquainted. Maria had
no intention of revealing any details of her recent
circumstances or disgrace to anyone; but of the balls she
had attended, the flirtations she had witnessed, the great
people she had encountered, she was pleased to talk, and
Lucinda was delighted to listen to her.

All the Lockley girls had been taught to ride as children,
and Lucinda acquitted herself well on the grey mare,
although her riding-clothes had been passed on from one of
her sisters and had none of the elegance of Mrs Rushton's.
Maria found that Lucinda needed little instruction and
their rides were sometimes long and agreeable to them
both. Lucinda was able to direct them along bridle-ways
and lanes hitherto unknown to her companion. One of

these led through the park of the manor and, on a slight rise, the girls reined in their horses to regard the house. It stood flanked by ill-tended shrubberies, a low quadrangular building in local stone, facing along its avenue of tumbled elms towards the village. "It is a pleasant old place," Maria remarked. "But I wish our elusive Mr Dalby joy of its condition. How long can it be since anyone inhabited it?"

"I do not remember that Mr Dalby – the late Mr Dalby – has come in my lifetime. Do you think the new Mr Dalby could want to live here? He would need to have a very large family, to fill such a house."

Maria said carelessly: "Oh, my husband's house was three times the size of this; and my father's bigger too. One does not reckon to fill a house with people. Indeed, the virtue of a spacious house is that one can get away from people." Turning her horse she rode on, and Lucinda followed, marvelling at what must have been the luxury of Mrs Rushton's earlier life, and more aware than ever of the privilege of associating with such a creature. Lucinda's simplicity was drawing her into some danger of confusing wealth with wisdom; she felt that no one with Mrs Rushton's dazzling experience of life could not have profited by it to advantage, and was ready to be impressed by any opinion Mrs Rushton uttered.

On a day soon after this, they rode up along a moorland track, and in the balmy sunshine Maria found the moors less desolate than she had remembered. They were returning along another lane, when Lucinda saw that by this route they would pass Ashcross farm. She would have liked to ask Mrs Rushton if she might visit Claudia, whom she had not seen since her visit of last year, and with whom the family's only communication had been through Mr Williams the curate. The messages he gave from Claudia were merely that she was well, and hoped everyone else was well; Lucinda did not doubt the messages but, had she dared ask Mrs Rushton to interrupt her ride, she would have been glad to confirm them for herself. But, as Mrs Rushton had already observed that they had been out for a long while, Lucinda said nothing. They were almost at the gates of the farmyard when Mrs Rushton said:

"This is a lonely place; what kind of people can think of living so far out of the world?" There was no sign of life, except for some geese that straggled about the lane; and, as Mrs Rushton spoke, a figure emerged from the yard and began to herd these together, trying to drive them into the gateway, which some of them, with stretched necks and rebellious cacklings, resisted. Mrs Rushton laughed. "That farm wench is having trouble with her flock," she pointed out. "Perhaps we should assist her?" And she guided her rather nervous horse to head off one errant bird.

"Keep that horse away," shouted the farm wench, whom Lucinda had already perceived to be Claudia. When the goose, dodging the hooves, had been chased after its fellows and the gate slammed on them, Claudia in turn recognised her sister, and Lucinda introduced her to Mrs Rushton. Claudia was joyful at the encounter.

"It has been for ever since I saw you. Why do you not ride up in this direction more often, now that you have such a splendid horse? "Thus Claudia, arms akimbo and cotton bonnet askew, hailed Lucinda. "Is it your own horse? Or I dare say, she borrows one of yours?" she added to Mrs Rushton, who nodded, indicating that such was the case. "Why do you not both come indoors, and take some tea? All the men are away at market and we are just finished with the baking."

Lucinda felt obliged to refuse the invitation, saying that she hoped to see Claudia again soon. As she and Mrs

Rushton rode away, she said:

"I have seen Claudia hardly at all since she married."

Coolly Maria returned: "I cannot blame you. Still, one can not be responsible for one's relations' choice of relations. It is as well your sister has moved as far as she has from home."

It had never ocurred to Lucinda to be ashamed of the Hodgson connection, little as she herself found it congenial. But the sense of shame, being implanted by Mrs Rushton, was not easily denied.

A Sunday intervened; then Mr Williams, calling at the Rectory on business, said to Lucinda with a smile: "I am to tell you, from Claudia, that you are not to act so much the lady when you next see her. What the message means, I do not intend to inquire."

"I wish you would tell Claudia –" began Lucinda with heat, before she recollected herself; she had wanted to say: Tell Claudia not to act so much the farm wench. She amended it to: "Tell Claudia I am grateful for her message, if you please." It was her desire that Mr Williams should think well of her, rather than any fear of a quarrel with Claudia, that made Lucinda temper her words. She had a high regard for Mr Williams's judgement as well as of his character. Of him, Mrs Rushton had once remarked when Lucinda referred to him: "Oh; the curate, yes. He is not a bad-looking man, but I do not know how he can bear with that terrible mother." And Lucinda did not protest that she herself was fond of Mrs Williams; she would not presume to set her opinions against those of Mrs Rushton. She said only:

"I wonder that he has not yet married."

"Probably she will not allow him to. Or possibly he is waiting until you are of suitable age."

"*I* marry Mr Williams?" cried Lucinda, in a

bewilderment that amused Maria. "How could I think of such a thing?"

"Come, you must learn to take a joke. You will do better than a country curate. You will marry for love or money, and live happy ever after."

"I wish I did not think that a joke also. I do not think I would marry for money, Mrs Rushton, either. I should think it wrong."

"Dear me, what a little prig you can be!" exclaimed Maria in some irritation. Lucinda at once apologised, but Mrs Rushton was continuing: "Money is not to be despised. In this world, it is at least the more durable of the two."

"I should hope that my love would prove durable, if it were fixed on someone I much admired," said Lucinda with resolution.

"Oh yes; provided of course that the beloved object equally admired you," returned Maria with a bitterness that Lucinda could not understand. She answered:

"I am sure I do not know that anyone could admire me."

"Do not be over-modest. You are a pretty enough girl, and as yet you have youth and virtue on your side. There is no reason yet why you should turn out like your sister. We must bring you out more. How would it be, if when I go to visit my sister, I take you with me, and introduce you to some fine young men, upon whom you may practise the arts of earning admiration?"

It was with conversations of this nature that Maria diverted her young friend as they rode side by side along the quiet lanes. As for visiting her sister, Maria had no real intention of doing so, nor of taking Lucinda with her if she did. The visit was a scheme she had invented in one of her quarrels with Mrs Norris, in order to make her aunt apprehensive. Her sister had not invited her, out of a certain respect for their father as well as out of a fear of receiving anyone proscribed by the society she moved in. Maria, in one of her fits of frustration, had declared that, were she to arrive unannounced at her sister's house, she could not be turned away; but it was not an experiment she seriously meant to try.

Lucinda, unaware of any of this, was elated by Mrs Rushton's offer, and pondered it in secret excitement. She said nothing of it at home. There was little indeed that she had to say at home nowadays; she did not find the Rectory comfortable and was grateful for the refuge of Ladysmead and the length of her rides with Mrs Rushton. When she had to be at home, the two young men intimidated her, Robert Davison by his studious silences and Peter Turner by his noise and chatter. Nor did Lucinda – seeing the situation increasingly as if through Mrs Rushton's eyes – feel it suitable that Sophia should be so often in an apron, performing the tasks for which Sally was too frail and the maids too forgetful under her direction. Sophia herself was too busy to listen much to tales of her sister's adventures, and, her nerves not improved by her immediate cares, she was not often in the mood.

It had added to Sophia's trials that, during the fine weather, and in the absences of Maria, Mrs Norris had begun to seek exercise and company by walking over to the Rectory to offer her advice and assistance to Miss Lockley. Of this, Mrs Norris could not but perceive that Miss Lockley was in need. She had seen, for instance, Peter Turner on a horse, galloping up the lane. Sophia had to pause in her search for mending cotton to explain that Mr Turner had hired a horse for himself, being desirous of exercise.

"But, my dear," cried Mrs Norris, "is he not here to study, and not to waste his time in gallivanting? My dear niece goes riding, as you may know, but that is not at all the same thing. Her health and spirits are the better for the fresh air. That young man should be at his books. I wonder your father does not check him.''

"My father does not find him punctilious in his studies, but I am afraid Mr Turner does not heed his reproofs.''

"Then it is for you to keep the young man to his duty. Your father cannot be chasing after him, with so many other affairs to attend to. And where is the horse stabled? I assume, you are charging for its keep. The price of oats is at present exorbitant. Hay will do very well. You must make sure the young man gives his horse only hay. I dare say your father's horses do not require oats, either. He does not ride them hard and it is only highly-bred animals, such as Mrs Rushton's, that should have special feeding.''

"You will excuse me, Mrs Norris, if I fetch something from the cupboard,'' said Sophia, remembering where she had last seen the cotton she needed. When she returned to the table with it, Mrs Norris proceeded at once:

"Are you about to mend that stocking yourself? One must make every effort, and make the most of everything, I know, but that stocking is in a very bad state. I should think your father would hardly wish to be seen wearing it. You must keep his clothing in respectable order.''

"This stocking is one of Mr Turner's,'' said Sophia, threading her needle.

"And are you to take such a task upon yourself? There are surely more important matters that you ought to be seeing to. Why cannot the maids do the mending?''

"Sally does a good deal of it, but her eyesight is poor. And the maids are busy today, because Sally wished them to take out and beat the bedroom carpets while the sun shines.''

"Indeed. That must explain that monstrous cloud of dust

that was coming from your yard as I approached the house. No doubt it is a long while since the carpets were beaten. They should, you know, be done at least once in two months. But, is Sally to be the one to decide what work is done about the house? You are the mistress, my dear, and if you do not make that plain there is no end to the liberties your servants will take."

Sophia said: "Sally has been with us all our lives, and we are fond of her."

"It is evident that she has been a very long while here," cried Mrs Norris, "from the age of the woman alone. I should guess she is well over seventy, is she not? I find her a heedless, uncivil old woman, myself, and if in addition she has failing eyesight the best thing you can do, Miss Lockley, is to turn her off, before she becomes utterly useless. I know how it can be with these old servants. One is tempted to keep them on, to do small tasks, and then, before one knows it, one is let in for tending them in their old age."

"We could not dismiss Sally. She has nowhere to go."

"Oh, my dear, that sort of person always has a niece, or a cousin, or someone who will take them in, if the truth is known. You must not let yourself be imposed upon. I understand that, if she was your nurse, you may feel you lack authority over her, but you must be firm. If you wish, and if you lack the courage, I shall speak to her for you."

"I must beg you not to do any such thing. My father might not be pleased. If ever it were to come to speaking to Sally, his is the authority, and no doubt he possesses the courage."

"No doubt he does," said Mrs Norris undaunted, "but you must not be running to your father with every little trouble that arises in the household. It is your duty to spare him from such concerns, and make his life tranquil.

Clergymen especially have great need of tranquility. My own dear husband had no idea of what was going on behind the scenes, so to speak, of his domestic peace."

"He was fortunate."

"Yes, though I say it myself, I have never been able to relax my efforts to make the lives of others more agreeable, cost me what it may have. I am not one to complain. My life has been entirely devoted to others and I am able to feel I have been the gainer thereby."

Possibly, Sophia thought, she had; but before she was forced to decide on a form of agreement that would not be ambiguous a sound of hooves had made Mrs Norris turn to the window: The horsewomen were returned, somewhat sooner than expected; scarcely bidding Sophia farewell, Mrs Norris hastened back to Ladysmead to welcome her dear niece.

Nine

As the weather deteriorated into that of a more normal English spring, Mrs Norris was less often at the Rectory since Maria, less often able to ride out, needed her to quarrel with. Peter Turner did not cease to ride, but tracked even more mud into the house. As Mrs Rushton was more often 'indisposed', Lucinda was more often at home, and less content to be so. Sophia, less able to contain her own discontent, did not gain by her sister's company, and even between these two there was occasionally a slight friction.

On one wet morning when Maria was desperate for occupation, she and her maid amused themselves by dressing Lucinda's hair in a style more in keeping with the current fashion. Lucinda saw herself transformed, and so did Peter Turner, who observed to Robert Davison while they were alone: "Do you know, that young sister – what's-her-name – when one comes to look at her, she is a deuced pretty girl. Odd, that I never noticed it before." He showed his awareness of this by an alteration in his manners, if not into gallantry, into a clumsy imitation of it. Lucinda did not like him any the better for the change. She complained of it to her sister and to Mrs Rushton, and from them received conflicting advice:

Sophia said: "Take no notice of him, Lucie. I do not think he means to be offensive, and if you remain polite but cool he will tire of the game."

Maria said: "So you have made a conquest? It is nothing to be annoyed about. It will be practice for you, in encouraging a suitor's attentions while keeping him in his place."

This, Lucinda felt incompetent to achieve; but guided by Mrs Rushton she let herself feel no shyness of Peter Turner, and rather enjoyed a new sense of power, in allowing him to see when he had pleased or displeased her. Her conduct did not strike her father or sister as out of the ordinary, because they were so far from imagining that Lucinda might be capable of anything like flirtatiousness. It was observed, however, by Charles Williams when he shared a family meal at the Rectory, and he was uneasy. A few days afterwards he chanced to meet Sophia, when both were on a charitable visit in the village, and he felt obliged to speak to her of Lucinda.

"Are you happy," he asked, "that Lucinda has been taken up in this way by the ladies at Ladysmead?"

"Lucinda is certainly happy about it. She is in their house at every opportunity."

"And what do you think of the influence of Mrs Rushton upon her? I know little of Mrs Rushton myself, but she would seem to come from a world very different from the one Lucinda has been used to."

"If you know little of Mrs Rushton, I do not see how you can foresee her influence," returned Sophia.

"I seem to detect it already. That is, I imagine it is from her, that Lucinda has acquired some of the ideas she expressed that evening; it is unlike Lucinda, indeed, to talk so much at all in company."

"Lucinda is sixteen; she cannot be a child for ever."

"No, naturally not. And she is growing up very prettily, and taking pains with her appearance. I like the style of her hair, but I confess, the lace she had trimmed on to her dress – it was, I understand, a cast-off from Mrs Rushton – I thought a little elaborate."

"I presume you do not wish me to pass on these flattering comments to Lucinda herself? She would be pleased to hear that you had studied her so closely."

"I do not suppose she would be much interested in my opinion. I had rather she depended on your taste than on Mrs Rushton's, and I am sure that, if influence is in question, yours will be the stronger."

"Then why trouble yourself to deplore Mrs Rushton's? I am sure I cannot help it, if Mrs Rushton is more fashionable than I am, and comes from a wider world, and has leisure to play the pianoforte and ride about on horseback on every fine day."

Sophia permitted herself a sharper mode of speech with Charles Williams than with anyone else. With him, she felt she could be as disagreeable as she felt inclined, and complain as bitterly as she liked. She had never asked herself why this should be so.

Quite unoffended, Charles said: "You know that fashion and leisure can be pitfalls, rather than aids, to the formation of character. I am convinced that Lucinda has all your own natural good sense, but I know also that you yourself are all too fully occupied nowadays to give her the attention you would wish. Might I venture a suggestion: that, as summer comes on, she be sent on a visit to your sister Mrs Merton, or elswhere, for a change of scene and interest?"

"An excellent suggestion. I thank you for it, Mr Williams. It occurs to you, of course, that elsewhere she should meet with more people of fashion and leisure than she can hope to in this confined area? The pitfalls might be multiplied. – And," she added with entire candour, "I expect Margaret would find her a husband, and she would go to live in London or some such place, and I should never see her again."

Charles Williams looked at Sophia with a compassion he dared not utter, and she, not raising her eyes to his, interpreted his silence, not without reason on her side, as conveying disapproval. Disguising her shame under anger, she said: "I thank you for your advice, Mr Williams. I am given a great deal of that. I am sorry I appear so much in need of it. Please give my compliments to your mother." And she walked quickly away.

During the time that it took her to walk home from the village, Sophia's natural good sense, which Mr Williams relied on, came to her aid, and she admitted that his suggestion had in truth been an excellent one; she should have thought of it herself, that Lucinda should go on a visit to Margaret, or Priscilla, or Aunt Sanderson in Liverpool; anywhere would serve to detach her from Mrs Rushton, whose taste in decorative lace trimming Sophia had in fact noticed and condemned though she could not remember what Lucinda had been talking of, to incur Mr Williams's displeasure when he came to supper; she supposed it had been some nonsense exchanged with Peter Turner, but no one else in the Rectory could talk nonsense to the boy and since it was all he himself could talk, it was as well that he should sometimes be indulged a little. Sophia reached home with restored composure and soon put her suggestion to Lucinda.

To her surprise, Lucinda rejected it. "I do not at all want to go away. I am quite happy as I am. Why should I go away?"

"Do you not want to see Margaret? And to have a change

of society? I thought you found our two guests tiresome –"

"Our guests are nothing to me. And I may not find a change of society lacking." Lucinda would not expand on this, but she was thinking of the invitation to the sister of Mrs Rushton. It would not do, to be away from home when that came.

For the same reason she refused another invitation which came, by coincidence, on the very next day: Emily Gray wrote to ask Lucinda to stay with her grandmother and herself, in their house in Kent, where they had been settled now for over a twelvemonth, and made many friends. This refusal surprised Sophia even more. "But you must be longing to see Emily again?" she urged Lucinda. "You were so close to one another."

"Yes, I dare say we were, but after so long a time we might find we had grown apart, and her new friends are probably as sober as she."

"They may be none the worse, for that."

"Oh, I understand you," cried Lucinda impatiently. "You do not like Mrs Rushton, nor that I should be so much with her. But I am old enough now to choose my own friends, and to form my own judgements. Mrs Rushton is kind to me, and amusing, which is more than I could say for everyone."

Sophia looked at her in astonishment. "That does not sound like my Lucie speaking. It is rather as Claudia used to be –"

"I shall not be like Claudia, thank you, and throw away my life for lack of choice in this neighbourhood."

Sophia thought it wiser not to enter into further argument, but she was saddened by Lucinda's attitude, and by the fear that any negligence of her own had fostered this estrangement between them. She did not believe, however, that estrangement between Lucinda and herself could go deep. She had known her youngest sisters since their infancy and felt she could assess their characters. Lucinda was flattered and dazzled by Mrs Rushton's attentions into behaving unlike herself; all this was merely a phase of her growing-up, and would pass. Sophia must be tolerant, and not provoke conflict that both would come to regret.

With this in mind, Sophia tried even to smile upon the closer friendship that seemed to be forming between Lucinda and the crass young Peter Turner. It was hardly a friendship; often, Lucinda snubbed or ignored the young man in such a manner that Sophia wondered at his persistence. She could only suppose that he was too stupid to recognise a rejection. It did not occur for a moment to Sophia that Lucinda could take the young man seriously as a suitor.

Mr Lockley had by this time ceased to take the young man at all seriously as a student. Not long ago, he had told Peter Turner that, if he did not intend to apply himself to work, he had better quit the house. This, Peter Turner did not at all like as an idea. He would have to go back to his parents, who would nag at him and perhaps send him off to some worse crammer; here, Peter was content for the moment, with the distraction of Miss Lucinda and the freedom of the countryside. He decided to mend his ways, to the extent of keeping quiet and out of the old fellow's way, surmising that his continued presence might not be noticed. The surmise was correct; Peter's simple wit had in this the measure of Mr Lockley, who was pleased by the progress of Robert Davison and, busy with him, barely observed that the other young man was still about the place. The general effect was that Peter Turner's behaviour in the house greatly improved and Sophia was more disposed to consider him oafish but harmless. When the

spell of bad weather at last ended, he was out of doors
nearly all day, and, as Mrs Rushton's rides had
recommenced, Lucinda was more away from the house too,
which afforded Sophia some relief.

She would have been less relieved, had she known that
Peter Turner was making it a practice to waylay Mrs
Rushton and Lucinda on their excursions. Mrs Rushton
did not discourage him; any lively company was a novelty
to her nowadays, and she was entertained by the flirtation
between the young pair. Often they rode for some distance
together, while Mrs Rushton provoked Peter into rash
declarations and Lucinda into a variety of arch replies.
Lucinda was amazed at herself, and enjoyed demonstrating
to Mrs Rushton that she could 'encourage a suitor while
keeping him in his place'. Peter too was amazed at himself,
that he could make someone of Mrs Rushton's quality
laugh; he imagined that she laughed at his wit, when she
laughed at his idiocy. The trio became quite pleased with
themselves and planned longer excursions for the summer,
across the moors to the ruins of a famous old abbey, or
down the river to an old mill town where there might be an
inn good enough for a meal.

They did not go unremarked. Empty as the country was,
news travelled about it, in the mysterious fashion that news
can, and from shepherd to tinker to farmwife to villagers
came the intelligence that the youngest Miss Lockley had
been gathering bluebells with her swain in Glebe Wood,
while the fine lady from Ladysmead rested in the sun by the
pond and the groom held the horses up by the gate. Sally at
the Rectory heard the story, but forebore to repeat it to
Sophia, who, Sally thought, would probably turn spoilsport
as she had over Miss Claudia. Charles Williams heard the
story and he too was reminded of the circumstances of

Claudia, but his reaction was different from Sally's; he was gravely disturbed.

He, too, decided not to tell Sophia, but this was because he did not want to alarm her. Instead, he set himself to patrol the country and keep watch on Mrs Rushton and her young friends, making it plain to them that he was doing so. In the ordinary way, Charles Williams performed most of the parish visiting. His manner with the countryfolk was easier, and he was more readily interested in their concerns, which often seemed trivial to Mr Lockley. The contribution that the latter most willingly made to the welfare of his flock was to shut himself in his study and compose sermons so full of abstruse exegesis and classical allusion that they passed over the heads of his congregations, who were none the less appreciative: the less they understood the sermon, these simple parishioners felt, the more good it must have done them spiritually; and possibly they were right.

However that may have been, it was Charles Williams's figure that was a familiar sight as he rode in all weathers about the considerable territory of the parish. It presented him with no great difficulty to arrange his journeys so as to meet up with Mrs Rushton's party. He might see them pass through the hamlet where his house stood, and calculate that they would be going through Manor Wood and that he might intercept them at the crossroads on his way to a certain farm; or, encountering them in the lane, he might inquire: "Are you going towards Brown Moss? I may see you; I must ride to Mrs Pease's later." Falling in with them, he would remark: "I hoped I should see you out, on such a fine day. May I join you, if you are on your way home?" He could scarcely be refused. After a little time it began to seem to them – as Mr Williams had hoped it

would – that, go where they might, they could never be sure
that the curate would not suddenly appear, over the skyline
or out of a wood.

Each interpreted the phenomenon differently. Peter
Turner thought the dismal old clergyman was just a nuisance, butting in where he was not wanted, and stopping most
of their fun. Lucinda felt that Mrs Williams might indeed be
keeping some sort of watch upon her, and was a little
gratified that he might think it necessary, because she had
hitherto had no idea of herself as a giddy young lady; she
would have liked to show him that so she was, but could not
help being a little subdued by his presence. Maria, still
finding the curate not a bad-looking man, took his
attentiveness wholly to herself, and imagined that she had
made a conquest, little worth making as it might be; she
was tolerant of the poor man and spoke to him with
condescending civility.

If it were mentioned at the Rectory incidentally, by
Lucinda or Peter Turner, that Mr Williams had ridden
alongside them between Brown Moss and Thornleigh
Farm, Sophia was reassured that the conversation must
have been rational and due order kept. She did not know
why sudden depression betrayed her into the recognition
that everyone except herself was free to range about the
summery landscape; she had never felt it so keenly before,
but it had for so long been so; she imagined that she might
be slightly unwell, and did in fact suffer frequently from the
headache, but would not permit herself to be, in the
manner of Mrs Rushton, 'indisposed'.

There was another witness, at second or third hand, of
Mr Williams's repeated encounters with the riding party,
who placed another interpretation on the matter, and that
was Mrs Williams, the curate's mother. The concentration
of her own life upon his welfare had always included the

wish that he should marry. She did not think that single men were ever truly happy, and was confident that she could get along very well with any wife of the right sort that he brought into the house; besides, she very much wanted grandchildren. As soon as her Charles was ordained and appointed to his curacy she began looking for a suitable wife for him, and decided that any one of the Rector's good-looking good-natured daughters would probably do very nicely. But on this one topic her son, normally so candid and communicative, was not approachable, and his mother had to watch the daughters of the Rectory one by one grow up, grow more suitable and then disappear. But now she was a little worried; Charles was over thirty, no new young ladies came upon the scene and the remaining daughter of the Rectory was devoted only to her father. It was not until Mrs Williams heard that her son was often in the company of the littlest girl and her friends that Mrs Williams took a closer look at Lucinda and admitted that she was a little girl no longer; she was suddenly a young lady and if anything the prettiest of them all. Hopefulness revived in Mrs Williams. She resolved to be very tactful with Charles, to ask no questions, but subtly to do all she could to bring about his union with Lucinda, whom Mrs Williams now admitted also to have been always a particular favourite of hers, and to be exactly the wife she would have chosen for her son: young enough to be tractable, handsome enough to please him, yet modestly enough brought up to have no ambitious expectations of life.

His mother's access of cheerfulness surprised but pleased Charles, who was himself despondent just now. He supposed that her rheumatism, that sometimes troubled her during the winter, had finally left her. When he inquired, she replied in powerful tones:

"Rheumatism?" at last catching the word. "No, I have not

felt a twinge for this long while. I feel excellently well, and I
have been thinking, Charles: I do not move about as much
as I should. No, I know, you tell me I should walk more,
and I agree, I become lazy. I should pay more visits in the
neighbourhood. I should like to see more of our friends at
the Rectory, and ask how they do. No, it is not at all too far
for me to walk. Yes, I would rest before walking home, of
course. I shall go tomorrow, if it is fair."

"That is good of you, Mother," said Charles. "I expect it
will cheer Sophia, to have your visit. I am afraid she is
sometimes lonely."

"Lonely?" cried Mrs Williams, seizing on that word, but
missing the name her son had spoken. "You and I, Charles,
must do what we can to remedy that. Such a charming
young girl must not fancy herself lonely. – Yes, we must
invite her to us, as well, quite soon."

Mrs Williams was disappointed next day to find Lucinda
from home, and Sophia was not immediately glad to have
to interrupt her morning's work and be bawled at for an
hour by Mrs Williams; but each made the best of it, and, as
they were naturally on good terms, each was the better for a
little change of company; till, on leaving, Mrs Williams
said:

"I know you are so busy, my dear, that I do not expect
you to return my call. Dear me, we are not on such formal a
footing as that, are we? No, but perhaps your youngest
sister may find time to come to see me? You will give
her that message. Thank you. I shall always be pleased to
see her. She is quite a young lady now, yes, and Charles
and I will like to hear how she does. Charles, I might tell
you in confidence, has quite an admiration for her. No, the
pleasure has been all mine – Thank you, my dear, and
good-morning to you."

Sophia having walked to the gate with Mrs Williams,

walked back telling herself: "She is a silly old woman, after all, and I am sure anyone of sense would admire Lucinda; she meant nothing, and I shall think no more about it." She went to the kitchen, to see how the baking of pies had turned out, and the heat of the stove brought on her headache.

Ten

Mr Mallet, the agent, was announcing all about the district the news that the missing heir to the Dalby estate had been found. He did live abroad, but the lawyers had been fortunate enough to locate him while he was on a visit to friends in the south of England. He had written to Mr Mallet from London, where he was engaged in the sorting out with the lawyers of his late great-uncle's affairs. When he had done so, he proposed to travel north and inspect his inheritance there.

Mrs Mallet was as busily putting it about that Mr Dalby had been invited to stay at the Mallet's house while he was in the region, as the manor-house could not be rendered habitable in time, should Mr Dalby even wish it to be. Mrs Mallet had pretensions to gentility, and let it be inferred that hers was the only dwelling in the district fit to accommodate a gentleman of Mr Dalby's status. No one gainsaid her; there was no great curiosity about Mr Dalby himself.

Maria said to Lucinda: "There will be your opportunity: You can marry this Mr Dalby, and reign as the lady of that tumbledown manor."

"Do you not think he may be already married?"

"I think nothing about him, and shall probably think as little when I meet him; if indeed I do."

As any dealings with lawyers were bound to involve delay, no one else thought more about Mr Dalby for the present. At the Rectory, more proximate, and troubling, topics had arisen; arising in the first place out of Lucinda's refusal to do as Sophia asked her and pay a visit to Mrs Williams. Lucinda voiced her objection in language that Sophia could not overlook:

"I do not see why I should visit that terrible woman."

"Lucie – Pray do not speak of her so. It distresses me, to hear you sound so hard and scornful, which you are not; and to hear you use such words."

"Well, I am sorry if you are distressed, but it seems to me that I speak no more than the truth. Besides, we are to go to Meldon Abbey, tomorrow or the next day, we have not yet decided."

"You, and Mrs Rushton, may I take it?"

"You may take what you please."

"That is generous of you. Will Peter Turner be of the party?"

"Very likely. I dare say you disapprove of that, too. You disapprove of all that I do nowadays. You are turning into a stiff old maid."

"I wish I could hope that no worse fate will overtake you," cried Sophia, "but you seem determined to turn yourself into a hard-hearted pleasure seeker, which can lead you to no possible good."

Too much had been said on both sides, and the sisters parted angrily. Sophia, on cooler but no sweeter reflection, began to ponder Lucinda's own hint, that she might disapprove of Peter Turner. Perhaps she should show more disapproval than she had. She decided to consult Sally.

"Sally," she asked the old woman, whom she found in

the dairy, "do you know whether Peter Turner and Lucinda meet often, outside the house?"

"Would I need to tell you? Everybody else knows that they go riding together. Them and that Mrs Rushton."

"I did not know that it was a regular practice. Does Mr Williams, do you know, often go with them?"

"So they say."

"I wonder that he has not mentioned it to me. He must know that I cannot like it, that Lucinda and Peter Turner should be too closely acquainted."

"Ah, well," said Sally with a knowing smile, "by what I hear, from that Mrs Norris' woman Nanny, Mr Williams has his own reasons for going riding with them."

"What can those reasons be, do you know?"

"Can you not guess? He finds Mrs Rushton a beautiful woman, I'm told, and he follows her about – He's not to be blamed; he cannot have met many ladies of her sort before."

It was preposterous to Sophia that she should be told within a week that Mr Williams had fallen into admiration of both Lucinda and Mrs Rushton. Of one or the other, she could have understood, but the confusion brought about by Sally's revelations drove her to exasperation. Glancing about the dairy she cried: "Sally! There is muslin for the cheese, thrown in a heap upon the floor. How can it have got there? It will not be fit for use."

"Muslin?" echoed Sally, also peering about. "Ah, yes; is that what it is? I was about to throw it away."

"But I gave it to you, when I had bought it, more than a week ago, and I told you to fold it and store it until it was needed."

"Ah, yes. I remember now, you did. But, with one thing and another, I brought it out here, meaning to put it somewhere on a shelf, and I must have forgotten."

"How can you be so careless? You see, it has been trodden upon, and had milk spilt over it – it will not stand the washing. It is wasted."

"Now, there is no need to scold at me lik that. Anyone can make a mistake. Your mother never spoke to me in that cruel way."

"When my mother was here, I am sure you were more competent in your work."

"For that matter, your mother was more competent in hers than one of her bad-tempered daughters whose name I need not speak," returned Sally.

Aware that in falling into undignified quarrel with Sally, she would not enhance her authority in the household or her own self-respect, Sophia fled the dairy, almost in tears. When she discovered that the drawingroom offered no refuge, because meanwhile Mrs Norris had arrived and awaited her there, Sophia was no quicker to regain her composure.

"Good morning," she said in evident agitation. "I am sorry, no one told me you were here. Please be seated – That is," since Mrs Norris was already seated, "may I offer you a glass of wine or –"

"No, I thank you. I have not come for refreshment. I am too busy for idle sociability, as you must be also. I am afraid, if you intend to make any use of that, you will be disappointed. How came it to be so spoiled?"

Following Mrs Norris's gaze, Sophia glanced down to see that she had entered the drawingroom with the length of dirtied muslin still in her hand. "This? Oh, no, it is of no use," she said, bundling up the muslin and turning to go and throw it away.

"Wait," said Mrs Norris at once. "Let me look at it. It may surprise you what can be done to remedy these mishaps."

"Nothing can be done for this. Sally has let it be trodden about the floor of the dairy for a week," said Sophia, petulantly.

"My dear, I have told you several times, you must turn off that stupid old woman. She must be wasting more time and money than anyone can afford, let alone anyone of such straitened means as yours. If you will heed my advice, which is given in the most helpful spirit, you will deal with her at once. Such an offence as this offers just the occasion for it. Your father would be bound to agree. You must go to her instantly, and tell her to pack her box. That will show her you are in earnest. You can later tell her that she may have a month's wages, if you can spare so much, to support her until she finds another situation – Not that she is fit for one, but she must do her best to find one, and let that be the end of it at last. Go along, do not hesitate; go along at once."

"No, indeed, Mrs Norris, I cannot –"

"Yes, indeed you can. Be quick about it. You must show your authority. You can not want to have the old woman in the house for an hour longer. It will look like weakness, if you do not deal with her immediately. You know you want rid of her."

In this moment's excitement of her nerves, Sophia felt she wanted Sally simply dead, which suppressed admission did nothing to brace her against the onslaught of Mrs Norris. Unable to defy or resist Mrs Norris, she abandoned what ramained of her dignity and, standing with the soiled muslin clutched in her hands, burst into tears. Mrs Norris's sympathy was more practical than consoling. She exclaimed:

"There, I knew it. You have not the firmness to take action when it is necessary. You are not experienced in commanding others. Stop crying. I shall help you. I knew it

would come to this in the end. I shall speak to your father."
And rising from her chair she went briskly out of the
drawingroom. Before Sophia could protest, Mrs Norris was
rapping at the door of Mr Lockley's study.

This was against all the rules of Rectory life. No one was
to disturb Mr Lockley in his work, except in dire
emergency, such as the house's being ablaze; which, from
the urgency of Mrs Norris's irruption, it might well have
been. "My dear sir," she cried, "here we must have your
voice on a serious matter. Your old servant Sally shows
herself incompetent and Miss Lockley has not the courage
to turn her away. It is my clear duty to ask your support for
her. When inefficiency and waste are undermining a
household, I cannot stand by and watch, without doing
what little I can to set matters right."

Mr Lockley had looked up from his book bewildered.
"Why," he asked, having brought his mind to the moment,
"what has Sally been doing?"

"Rather, it is what she has not been doing. She has been
useless this long while. She is too old for work, and careless
besides. In your kindness of heart, you have all tolerated
her, but now it is in your best interest to make an end. She
is slatternly, uncivil and lazy, and Miss Lockley can no
longer control or suffer her."

Mr Lockley had no idea of any of this. He looked beyond
Mrs Norris and saw Sophia standing in the doorway,
clearly distressed, with tears on her face, and was himself
distressed by her unhappiness. "What is the matter, my
dear Sophia?" he asked her.

"The matter is," replied Mrs Norris before Sophia could
speak, "that this old woman has tormented her beyond
bearing, and must be got rid of at once."

"Let Sally be sent for," said Mr Lockley, roused to
decisiveness by Mrs Norris's own. "I shall hear what she

has to say for herself."

"Oh, my dear sir, there is no need of that. There is nothing she can say that can excuse her. You may leave it to me, to tell her what has been decided." And, calling the housemaid who lingered in the hallway to overhear the cause of this unusual disturbance, Mrs Norris commanded that Sally be brought quickly to her master's study.

Sophia attempted to intervene. "Please, Father, I do not think Sally can be treated as severely as Mrs Norris suggests. She is old, and –"

"Do not listen to Miss Lockley," cried Mrs Norris. "She will weaken, and it is to her credit that she pities the old woman, but one can not afford to be soft-hearted in running a household."

As Sally approached, Sophia felt she herself could take no further part in the scene. In a confusion of emotions she could only whisper to Sally as she passed her: "Be apologetic, Sally –" before withdrawing to her own room, to repair her appearance and calm herself. It was not long before Sally followed her there, weeping. Sophia understood that Sally had tried to be apologetic, but had not been listened to, and that she had been summarily dismissed.

"Thirty years, nearly, I have given to your family, and now to be thrown from the door like a stray dog, to starve – Your mother would never have treated me so – I do not know how you can be so wicked –"

"Listen to me, Sally," said Sophia with new resolution. "It is not my intention at all that you shall be sent away, and I do not believe that my father, had he been given time to reflect, would have been so harsh. I shall appeal to him, when Mrs Norris is absent, and I am sure he will listen to me."

"Oh, Miss Sophia, if you would do that, I should bless

you all my life. Be apologetic, you told me, and little use
that was, not a word was I let to speak, and no chance at all
to stand up for myself – But to you my dearest Miss Sophia,
I am apologetic, truly I am, and I admit my faults, and I am
sorry for them all, and if you will not send me away, I will
never again forget to tell you that the knifegrinder has
been, or give away eggs to Betty Robbins ..." And the poor
woman began to pour out a confession of all the offences she
had committed against Sophia, harking back even to the
deceptions she had practised during the courtship of
Claudia and Joseph Hodgson, and referring to the present:
"... and about Miss Lucinda and this young Mr Turner, I
expect it is all gossip I hear, but what I hear, this time, I
will not keep from you –"

"But, Sally," cried Sophia in alarm," what could there
be to tell me?"

"Well, there is nothing, only about how they go off
together when they are supposed to be riding, and that Mrs
Rushton, her man tells Nanny, she as good as gets them to
flirt with each other shamefully. I thought you would be
angry, if I told you, and I hoped there was no harm in it,
but if you are to take my part with your father I will take
your part too, from this time on, and so I promise you."

Sophia, her estimation of her father in this case
coinciding with Peter Turner's, advised Sally to keep out of
her master's sight meanwhile, in the hope that he would
become absorbed in his work and forget this morning's
episode until Sophia could speak to him at a suitable
moment. Sophia herself was so much disturbed by what
Sally had said of Lucinda and Peter Turner that Sally's
own plight lost importance. She reproached herself sternly,
for allowing Lucinda to be led into such indiscretion, and
could not see how worse could be prevented. When she had
sent Sally back to her work – or, more probably, to lament

her woes in the kitchen and hinder the work of the rest of the servants – Sophia came downstairs to find the house quiet. Mrs Norris had gone; her father was shut into his study again, and Robert Davison shut into his own room; Lucinda and Peter Turner were out; out, wondered Sophia, where? She had a desire fostered by an apprehension that was near to panic, to go out and seek them and discover for herself how they were conducting themselves.

The morning was now far advanced and, after its disruption, Sophia felt that in any case to go out of doors would soothe her. Dinner should be in hand and there was nothing she might not neglect for an hour or so. She determined to pay Mrs Williams the call that Lucinda had refused, attracted in part by the idea of walking through the woods. There was a pleasant green path that, leaving the Rectory lane, rounded a spur of wooded ground above the village and emerged close to the Williamses house, half-way between the village and the manor house. Today it was dry and shady, and its peace and her solitude enabled Sophia to perceive the best solution to the problem: Peter Turner had to be sent away, whatever the loss to the Rectory's income. He must not be allowed to remain in the proximity of Lucinda. Then perhaps the gossip that the Rector's youngest daughter was a flirt would naturally die.

The prospect of approaching her father with both requests – that he keep Sally and send away his pupil – made Sophia the more grateful for this interval before she need do so, and she looked forward to a brief visit to Mrs Williams with unusual pleasure. The curate's house was small, little more than a cottage, but compactly and tidily furnished, its garden bright with flowers. Mrs Williams, sewing at a table in the front window, saw Sophia, and came herself to the door, beaming welcome. When they entered the little drawingroom Sophia was surprised to see that Charles Williams was also there, busily writing at the central table.

"I thought you would be out, at this time of day," she told him.

"I must go out very soon, but first I have letters to write." He brought a chair for Sophia, placing it near his mother's, so that Sophia should be close enough to make herself heard by Mrs Williams, were she afforded a chance to speak. Mrs Williams was in full voice:

"Are you tired from your walk? Of course not; at your age, a mere mile or so is nothing. No, I do not find it tiring, either, to walk as far as the Rectory, and it did me good, the other day, to have the exercise. You would like some refreshment? Charles, yes, bring that Madeira we were given by Mr Greenhalgh. Miss Sophia would like a little Madeira." Sophia shook her head to Charles, who nodded that he would accept her refusal of the wine. She indicated that he should continue with his letters, and he seated himself again at the table and took up his pen. Meanwhile Mrs Williams was proceeding: "I hope your sisters are all well, and your father? I am glad. Do you hear that Mr Dalby is to come from London? Yes, everybody has heard. Will he settle here, or will he sell up the estate? No one knows yet. This house is on his property, you know. It is not a church house. Charles and I would be hard put to it, to find another that would do us as well, but it may be that, soon, we shall be in need of a larger house, in any case." She paused there, to give Sophia a significant glance, which Sophia, inattentive, did not try to interpret. During the pause Sophia said to Charles, who instead of writing was intently regarding her:

"Do finish your letters. You must not disappoint Mrs Rushton."

Charles could not imagine what she meant by that, but,

recollecting himself, he drew his paper towards him. "If you will excuse me, I shall just finish this one ... It is kind of you to visit us," he added, "and I am glad you could find the leisure, for a walk on such a fine day."

"It was not such a fine day within doors. That is why I made the leisure. Mrs Norris called, and is making my father turn off Sally, and he will do so, unless I can prevent it."

"Surely he could not do that; what would become of her, at her age?" askd Charles, with concern. Mrs Williams observing that they had entered on conversation, nodded and smiled, agreeing with them both.

"I am afraid he could, with Mrs Norris to persuade him. She is not a person to be easily withstood. I wish those ladies had never come to Ladysmead. They have made nothing but trouble. Not, of course, that I can expect you to agree with me in that."

Charles did not offer any disagreement; his mind was still on old Sally. "If she is indeed dismissed the Rectory, and has nowhere to go, my mother and I could have her here. We should not see her in want." And he rose to go closer to his mother, to explain the question into her ear.

"Certainly," exclaimed Mrs Williams when she had heard him. "If poor old Sally is homeless, we shall make a place for her. She is not of much use in her work lately, as anyone can see, but Lucinda might be glad to have her, so it could all be for the best."

The reference to Lucinda, both Sophia and Charles disregarded, supposing that Mrs Williams had imperfectly understood. Sophia said to Charles:

"Your idea is absurd. This house is cramped already, and you could not crowd another person into it."

"We should contrive to. I assure you. We would not wish to see old Sally turned out of doors."

"I thank you for the implication that *I* should wish to."

Charles protested at once that he had intended no such implication, but Sophia ignored him, turning from him to take from her basket the cinnamon cakes she had brought, as the only thing to hand, as a gift for Mrs Williams. Mrs Williams was delighted with the present and insisted that she must cut some flowers from her garden for Miss Sophia. She hustled out at once to find her bonnet and scissors, leaving the other two in a silence momentarily awkward.

"I think you might have warned me," Sophia began, "that Lucinda was carrying on a flirtation with Peter Turner. I am now told that the whole neighbourhood knows of it."

"I did not want to trouble you. I have been doing what I can, to keep a watch on them."

"It does not seem to have been to much effect. Perhaps you have had distractions, during your vigilance. Nor do I see why you should have taken it upon yourself to supervise Lucinda's affairs, instead of telling me of them. I should not have expected you to be underhand with me."

Charles, without attempting to justify himself, said: "Perhaps I was mistaken, in taking the course I did. I do not think great harm has yet resulted to Lucinda –"

"Except that she has become the target for the gossip of the whole district, no, I dare say no great harm. But now that I know of it the whole thing is to be stopped."

"There I agree with you. Lucinda has been led astray. Peter Turner is a foolish young man and I have been surprised that Mr Lockley is pleased to have him remain in his house."

"He is not, I hope, likely to remain."

"No – He should be sent away."

"Exactly the proposition that had occurred to me."

"I am sure your father will concur. If not, would you like

me to speak to him? I could tell him what I have observed myself of the affair –"

"I have already had enough, thank you," cried Sophia, "of people speaking to my father on my behalf. It seems, I am to have no voice of my own, and am never considered competent in anything –"

At this, Charles began to conradict her with some vehemence, but he was immediately interrupted by the reappearance of his mother. "Come, my dear," she boomed at Sophia, "you shall show me what flowers you like best, and we shall make up a pretty nosegay for you, and one for you to carry to Lucinda." Sophia went with alacrity, to follow Mrs Williams round the garden, to be asked what flowers she preferred, told, and to hold them when they were cut, and to return home without going into the house again or saying farewell to Charles Williams.

Eleven

Mr Lockley would have reckoned, had he considered it, that his daughter Sophia had a fairly easy life. Other young women of her age ran larger households, with the added responsibility of children; he himself was punctilious in his ways and made few demands upon her. Lately, she had been improving. She had been less extravagant and he had not had to reproach her with anything like the lack of vigilance she had shown in the unfortunate case of her sister Claudia. Sophia should by now be more contented, in the awareness of duty better fulfilled.

So, being shown that she was not happy, he was perplexed, but felt compunction. After cogitation, he asked her to come to his study, on the day following the dismissal of the old nurse:

"Sophia, my dear, I wish to speak to you."

"Yes, Father. I was going to ask if I might speak to you too."

They regarded one another across Mr Lockley's table with its stacked tomes. "I do not wish to be unsympathetic to you, Sophia. If Sally was troubling you, it is right that she should leave. But you should have complained to me of her sooner."

Sophia now had to explain that Sally was still here, and that she hoped her father would let her stay. Mr Lockley was doubtful. Sophia added: "It may be that we shall have the charge of her in her old age, but is that not our charitable duty?"

The appeal to principle was effective. Mr Lockley saw that Sally must remain. Sophia now had to proceed to her request that Peter Turner should not.

"Since you say that I should complain to you, I am afraid I must do so, about Peter Turner. I should be glad if he were to leave the house. "She had carefully prepared her reasons for this, hoping to draw as little as possible of her father's reproof on Lucinda, of whose indecorum he was probably even unaware; no one in the parish was less likely than its Rector to take part in its gossip. But as Sophia drew breath to give her reasons Mr Lockley simply replied:

"So should I. He does no work for me, and idles away his time. I have told him before now, that if he showed no improvement he must leave. He has shown none to me. Nor, I infer, to you?"

"None, Father."

"Then I shall tell him today, that he must go. Please send him to me as soon as he can be found."

Sophia had not suspected that her father had previously warned Peter Turner that he might be sent away; to her great relief, she realised that she need not mention Lucinda in this connection. The interview with her father had passed off more easily than she had dared to hope.

Sophia may have been relieved, but Mr Lockley was left still in a faint perplexity; he could not account for this; merely to have had his seclusion broken into at all left ripples of disturbance in his mind. He was never indecisive; he took his pen now and wrote to Peter Turner's father, before he had informed Peter himself of his banishment.

In informing Peter, Mr Lockley offered no scope for plea or excuse. The letter went to the post and Peter's boxes were brought out to be packed. Peter, privately admitting that his dismissal was overdue, took little time to regret his fair Lucinda. There would be other pretty girls in other places; what bothered him more was what his father would say to him when he arrived home. Peter decided that university was a waste of time anyway and that he might join the army.

Lucinda, when Sophia told her that Peter was going away, said nothing, in order to deny Sophia any triumph over her. Indeed, Lucinda was not more sorry than Peter about their separation. She had no affection for him and looked forward to a more peaceful time in having Mrs Rushton to herself again. When she carried the news of Peter Turner's departure over to Ladysmead, however, she chanced to do so at a moment wherein Mrs Rushton was slightly indisposed, and was upon the sofa, disposed only to find fault with the world.

"So they have sent your lover away, my poor creature. There is always someone in a hurry to spoil one's happiness."

"I hope," cried Mrs Norris from her work-table, "that remark is not directed at me, Maria dear. No one could do more than I do, to secure happiness for you."

"My remark was directed only at Lucinda, whose father seems, like mine to want to commit her to a life of rustic tedium."

"My sister says," ventured Lucinda, "that my father sent Peter away because he was bad at his studies, and not because he knows anything at all about Peter's association with me."

"Oh yes; your sister. Trust me, she will have been at the bottom of it. I dare say she is jealous and does not want you to have admirers."

"It is true, Sophia does not like what she has heard, about Peter and me."

"And what can she have heard?" put in Mrs Norris. "Why should young people not go riding together, properly chaperoned?"

"Miss Lockley may think me an improper chaperone," suggested Maria in an indifferent voice.

Mrs Norris was incensed. "How dare she suppose that? Who could be a better judge of conduct, or guide to young persons, than you, my dear?" This, Mrs Norris sincerely believed. "If Miss Lockley has any fault to find, it had better be with herself, for not taking care of her younger sister, and going about with her herself, if she is so particular about her company. I am sure Miss Lockley is in no position to criticise *you*."

"Miss Lockley may criticise me as much as she wishes," returned Maria, yawning, "if it pleases her to do so. But she ought not to be so petty as to separate Lucinda from her only male society."

Lucinda began to feel her own resentment of Sophia rising. "She did say that she was sorry if I should miss Peter, but I did not answer. I expect she is pleased, really, that I am without him. But I do not see what I can do. He is gone, and I shall never meet him again."

"If this were in a novel, you would run away with him to Gretna," suggested Maria.

"But I do not in the least want to marry Peter, Mrs Rushton."

"There, I respect your taste. – Then, you would pine, and grow pale, and presently hang yourself from the belfry of your father's church."

"I do not in the least want to hang myself, either. Besides, this is not in a novel. All I want is to be able to ride out with you again, as we used to."

"Well, you cannot; my horse is gone lame. And your charming curate would probably pursue us, as usual. There is no peace anywhere."

"Yet you were just saying, dear Maria, that life was tedious," Mrs Norris reminded her.

"And so it is. The only excitement I can foresee is that Lucinda shall hang herself. But upon the whole I hope she will not, because life would be insufferably more tedious without her. Of the two, I had rather see Miss Lockley dangling from the church tower."

"Yes, Miss Lockley has been chiefly at fault, in all this," readily took up Mrs Norris, who had not forgiven Sophia after discovering that Sally was still in the Rectory. "She is weak in giving way to an old servant, but strict enough when it comes to using her sister cruelly. I am surprised, Lucinda, that you do not assert yourself more against her. If you will take my advice, you will not let her order your life for you, or criticise your friends."

Lucinda took this advice so far as to decide, on her way home, that she had not behaved so far as befitted a young lady cruelly separated from her lover. When she reached home she locked herself in her bedroom and set herself to pine. She did not find it difficult. With Mrs Rushton's horse lame, and Mrs Rushton out of humour, and no Peter to tease, there was little to look forward to in life.

Sophia, when Lucinda would open the door to her neither that day nor the next morning, was anxious.

"Lucie," she called, "please let me see you. Are you ill?"

"What else should I be," called back Lucinda, "ill-used as I am?"

Sophia went to consult Sally. "I wish you would ask her to unlock her door. She may do so for you, if not for me."

Lucinda, hearing Sally's voice, relented and let her in. She was weakened, from having had no food in twenty-four hours, but when she asked Sally to bring her some milk and bread Sally answered: "If you want bread and milk, miss, you may come downstairs and fetch it for yourself." Sally then went downstairs and told Sophia: "Old and foolish I may be, but I did not nurse you all for nothing, and I still know a childish sulk when I see it. Nothing ails her."

If Sophia was a little reassured by this diagnosis, Lucinda, feeling that her last friend had failed her – for she had always been able to count on Sally's comfort against Sophia's censure – began to feel ill in earnest. For several days she lost all her appetite and began to need the ministrations of her sister and Sally and to cause them some concern. Lucinda herself hardly knew what would revive her, except the promised visit to Mrs Rushton's sister. Only on this could she fix any hope of restored health and happiness. But, although she seemed to hear Mrs Norris's voice in the house once more, she was not told that anyone from Ladysmead had so much as inquired after her.

Mrs Norris just now, virtually banished from her own house, was making a habit of visiting the Rectory in order to offer her advice there. Maria was in a continual fit of temper, over the loss of her horse and of Lucinda, and even Mrs Norris felt she might be better sometimes left alone. Moreover, since her encounter with Mr Lockley Mrs Norris felt increasingly obliged to see to his interests, perhaps more so as she had not gained her point over the dismissal of the old servant. Mr Lockley was much surprised that the lady waylaid him as he mounted his horse, or even rapped again at the door of his study, to inform him of some remedy she had suggested for a deficiency of his domestic affairs. She addressed him with many apologies for the taking up of his valuable time, and with assurances that her ideas were exactly what she knew he would have put forward himself, had he had time to attend to such details, and in all with such combination of importunity with flattery that Mr Lockley, still perplexed, could not rebuff her. The self-absorption that had been closing about him since the loss of his wife required a vigorous shock for its cracking, and no one was better equipped to administer this than Mrs Norris. He was in the way of coming, if not to rely on her advice, at least to recommend Sophia to do so.

The more frequent intrusions of Mrs Norris, and Lucinda's malady, made the house no more peaceful to Sophia for Peter Turner's absence. Charles Williams calling for the third time in three days found her harassed.

"My mother," he said, "sends me again to inquire after Lucinda."

"Your mother is very particular to inquire after Lucinda. Could you not make her hear that Lucinda is not gravely ill?"

"My mother has a great affection for her. She is, I hope, better?"

"In fact, I think so. She was downstairs upon the sofa for some time last evening. Sally maintains still, she is merely fretting for Peter Turner, or wishes us to believe so."

"I hope that is not true. If it is, she had better not be so much alone. Is she not fit for her rides with Mrs Rushton yet?"

"Sally says Mrs Rushton is not riding out; as you yourself are probably aware."

"I have not seen her lately, it is true. Is she not well?"

"If she were not, I am sure her aunt would inform us. And if she were not, I am sure her aunt would stay more at home; an illness of Mrs Rushton's, I should in that way be grateful for."

"Does Mrs Norris visit you often?"

Sophia answered this only with a shrug. Charles Williams resumed: "I heard some news just now that may cheer you a little: I met Mr Mallet, and he tells me Mr Dalby is expected here within a week or two."

"Why should that cheer me? I have no curiosity about this famous Mr Dalby, nor do I suppose I shall encounter him while he is in the area." Sophia would have been surprised had she been told, that she and Mrs Rushton expressed themselves so similarly on this topic.

Charles Williams went home to tell his mother that Lucinda was now said to be improving. Mrs Williams was glad to hear it, though she had been equally glad to send Charles daily to the Rectory on the excuse of Lucinda's illness. It had only recently come to Mrs Williams's knowledge that Lucinda Lockley had been flirting about the countryside with one of her father's pupils. Mrs Williams was fond of gossip, but few people had the patience to make it audible to her. She received together the items that the flirtation had been going on and that the young man had been sent away and a stop put to it. She would have expected her son to be pleased about this, although he must have been cast down by Lucinda's not being well; from what his mother could observe of his mood, however, it was steadily gloomy nowadays. Pondering his condition, Mrs Williams was forced almost to a conclusion she loyally would not admit to herself: that if little Lucinda were capable of flirtation, and perhaps delicate in health, it was a pity that it was with her that Charles had fallen in love. It was a pity he could not fall in love with Sophia, who would upon the whole be more suitable for him, and whom Mrs Williams herself found easier company.

Twelve

If Sophia had hoped not to meet Mr Dalby, it seemed that she was to be disappointed. Mrs Mallet called at the Rectory to explain that she intended to give a small dinner-party for the new owner of the estate, while he was staying at her house. "A select party, you understand me, Miss Lockley – highly select. Just your father and yourself, and the Jarrolds, and my sister will be staying with us, which will make the numbers even. I feel, if you understand me, that I should make some gesture of hospitality, since the gentleman is quite a stranger, and, however high his notions may be, no one could object to a clergyman and a doctor? Both so respectable. And my sister, of course, is the widow of a gentleman who was in a very good way of business in Manchester. On the other hand, you must understand me, we know absolutely nothing of Mr Dalby, and he may turn out to be – We know of course that he is a gentleman, but he has lived abroad, and there are some strange places abroad, would you not agree? He may be quite uncouth. In case of that, one must not overwhelm him with society, and I think, do you not, that a select dinner-party such as I am arranging will be satisfactory to him."

Sophia readily undertook that she and her father would

not overwhelm Mr Dalby. The party had been planned for the evening following Mr Dalby's arrival, since it was not supposed that he would be for long in the district.

Mrs Norris, hearing of this, cried: "I hope indeed that he will be long enough in the district for me to show him the disgraceful condition of Ladysmead. I deem it no great honour to dine at the Mallets' – though from the sound of it, the evening will be dull for a man of taste, if such he be – but I declare that I have tired myself out, chasing after Mr Mallet and describing the state of the pantry wall, and nothing has yet been done."

"Perhaps," Sophia reminded her, "if Mr Dalby means to sell the estate – and Mr Mallet thinks he may – he will not wish to be involved with details of its upkeep."

"You would not call it a detail, my dear Miss Lockley, if you had to live with it, as I have. Your own walls, even, are in better condition. All your pantries need is whitewashing – I should have mentioned that to you, but yesterday I forgot, having to hurry home on account of the doctor's visit. My niece, I am thankful to say, tells me he declared her in very good health. If Mr Dalby does sell the estate," she added, "let us hope it will be to someone who employs an agent more capable than your friend Mr Mallet. I am sure I wish you a delightful evening with him and this man of whom we have heard so little. He may prove to be acceptable, though from his curious circumstances I am disposed to doubt it."

Whatever the doctor had said of Mrs Rushton's health, the farrier's report on that of her horse now equalled it, and Mrs Rushton sent her groom to the Rectory with a message, requiring Miss Lucinda to ride with her tomorrow. The effect of the message on Lucinda's health was promptly restorative and she insisted on obeying the summons, but she returned home very much tired and without Sophia's urging, went to bed at once. Sophia was afraid the exertion had been too much, after her sister's recent inactivity, and some of her fear for Lucinda's health revived; it had to be admitted in Mrs Rushton's favour that, since Lucinda had ridden with her, Lucinda had been growing stronger and her complexion gained colour. It was to be hoped that she would find today's fatigue only temporary and recover more strength soon.

Lucinda did not disclose to her sister that her fatigue arose mainly from disappointment: Mrs Rushton had not been in a good humour today, had not referred to any visit to her sister and had had little to say at all, except once or twice glancing about, to remark that she was glad that dull curate was not still following them.

Mr Lockley and Sophia, setting out for the Mallets', left Lucinda in bed and Robert Davison to dine alone, to which that young bookworm did not at all object. The Mallets' house stood some way beyond the village, facing the Bardton road, so the cob had to be harnessed to the trap that Mrs Norris considered below a clergyman's dignity. The drive itself, dignified or not, was pleasant to Sophia. It was haytime, with roses in the hedges and swallows skimming the ponds, and, for the first time since she had dined at Ladysmead last autumn, she was to be offered a meal that she had not had to order and supervise herself. This was enjoyment enough; her expectations of pleasure were moderated now by her life's routine, and did not attach themselves highly to the evening's society.

So, on meeting Mr Dalby, she felt no disappointment, although at first sight he was not an unusually impressive figure. He was quite a young man, possibly under thirty, and slightly built. His dress was neat without being over-fashionable, and his manners gentlemanly. In his speech, there was an intonation that might have grown upon it from his long use of foreign language. If there were a Mrs Dalby, he had not brought her north with him. As he was presented to Sophia, and bowed, he raised his eyes briefly to hers, and a glint of intelligence in his as he politely smiled suggested to Sophia that she was being rapidly appraised. She felt that Mr Dalby, self-effacing as he might appear in this assembly, was no fool.

At the dinnertable, he was not permitted to efface himself; he was, after all, the guest of honour, as well as the newcomer, and his history and future were of interest to everyone present, with the probable exception of Mr Lockley and Mrs Oldshaw, the sister of Mrs Mallet. Sophia had met this lady on earlier visits, and found her stiff and silent. She sat unresponsive to the conversation and might have been as deaf as Mrs Williams or as bored as Mrs Rushton, but Sophia fancied that she was afflicted only with some mixture of pride and diffidence.

It was for the most part Dr Jarrold and Mrs Mallet who led the interrogation of the stranger. To their questions, he yielded piece by piece the information that he had lived for the past four years in New York (which, he explained to Mrs Mallet, was in North America) and that before that he had lived in Montreal for a time; he had left England when he was only twenty, and been abroad for nine years (at this, mental arithmetic was visible in Mrs Mallet's contracted brow) and that he had been astounded, when on a visit to some old friends in Brighton, to read in the newspaper that he was required to make contact with the lawyers of his great-uncle.

"I had never met him," Mr Dalby proceeded, submitting to the general desire to hear his family story, and talking more fluently; as if, Sophia imagined, to get the story told and done with and oblige his hearers. "He had, I was once told, quarrelled with my grandfather, his brother, and he was never mentioned in our family. My own family consisted only of my parents, one sister and myself. It was tragically that I was separated from them: my father, mother and little sister were all killed when the house caught on fire one night. At the time, I was at boarding school, and twelve years old. My aunt – my mother's sister – then took charge of me, and to her kindness I owe what happiness I was able to regain. My grandfather – and much less my great-uncle – showed no interest in me. Nor did I concern myself with them. I would have supposed, had I thought about it, that my great-uncle would have willed his property to relatives of his wife's side of his family. He married, the lawyers say, a widow, who had daughters; but she died soon afterwards. What became of the daughters, the lawyers do not know; they count themselves lucky to have found out what had become of me. I have asked them to do what they can to trace my great-uncle's stepchildren, but they say I have no legal duty towards them. Nevertheless, I hope they may not be in want. All this has caused me so much delay, when I originally intended to return to New York last month, that I almost think of altering the course of my life, and remaining in England. This depends, of course," he added with candour, "on what the value of my great-uncle's property turns out to be, by the time the lawyers have finished all their complicated toil. Mr Dalby left enormous debts, but he owned, I find, a coal-mine in Nottinghamshire, as well as his London house, and, I am most gratified to discover, this delightful estate, of whose existence I had never even heard."

And, assuming a more cheerful tone, Mr Dalby began to speak in praise of this countryside, with an enthusiasm that could admit no doubt of his sincerity. "It attracts me strongly. Even after four and twenty hours in the district, I can picture myself making my home here, very much to my own surprise. I had not expected it to be so beautiful."

Mrs Mallet said: "We who have to live here think the scenery apt to be dull and wild. But it may be that, where you come from, in New York, it is even more backward?"

Mr Dalby was amused. "Why, no, Ma'am; New York reckons itself to be a very fine city, and justifiably. I have seen some country while I was travelling about Canada, however, that makes this area appear as tame as a pleasure-garden."

Dr Jarrold asked him what had taken him to Canada originally at so young an age. Mr Dalby explained with the same frankness that he had not been a distinguished scholar by any means, and that although after leaving school he had taken the advice of his uncle and aunt, and began to study law, he had found that difficult and tedious. Falling in with a fellow-student of like mind, he had decided to invest the small amount of money left to him by his father in travelling to Canada in order to prospect for gold. The two of them had had many adventures but no success in their project, and after a while had had to find employment with a company that traded in furs. Presently they had secured an agency of their own, and removed to New York with the ambition of setting up a business there. "Which," ended Mr Dalby, "we are, in a small way, at last beginning to render profitable."

"And what would become of that business," pursued Dr Jarrold, "if you were to remain living in England?"

"Why, sir, that depends still upon the amount I possess when my great-uncle's affairs are settled. I had thought, if the result were good, of buying out my partner, and moving west, perhaps to Chicago, to start out on my own. That is what I should have wished, had I the capital. But now, as I say, my plans are thrown into disarray by the temptations of this delightful country property that I now find to be mine."

"It may require more of your capital than you think, to set the estate in order," remarked Dr Jarrold.

Mr Mallet hastened to put in: "It has been difficult – virtually impossible to manage the estate as it should be, recently. I have had difficulties, in the absence of Mr Dalby, and his neglect –"

"That is evident," said the younger Mr Dalby, not unkindly. "The manor-house is pretty well uninhabitable, for a start. But it is a fine old house of its period, and should be worth restoring. I met a friend while I was passing through London, who, from my scanty description, said he would be interested in buying it, and I almost said he would be welcome to do so, but reserved my consent until I had seen the place for myself; which I am now glad that I did. I am much interested in it for myself."

After this, Mr Dalby applied himself to eating, having fallen behind the others with his recital, and left them to digest his information and their own food. The dinner was good, but Sophia was able to observe some anxiety in Mrs Mallet at some stages of the serving; she could sympathise. When the dessert was brought in, there was some frantic whispering with the maid during which 'pineapple' could be overheard, but no pineapple appeared. In the drawingroom, Mrs Mallet favoured the ladies with an account of the pineapple's mishap until the gentleman joined them. When they did, Sophia took it as no great compliment to herself that Mr Dalby made instantly for a chair beside hers. In all modesty she felt that, with the fussiness of Mrs Mallet, the stiffness of Mrs Oldshaw and the insipidity of Mrs Jarrold, competition among the female company was not formidable to herself.

"I have talked of nothing but myself for the last couple of

hours," he addressed her pleasantly. "Much as that subject absorbs me, I find it as agreeable to turn to others. Tell me, Miss Lockley, do you appreciate this countryside as I do? Or do you, like our hostess, find it dull and wild?"

Sophia admitted that, during the winter, it could appear so. He asked her how she then amused herself, whether she was fond of reading, what books and poets were her favourites; he inquired about the extent of her father's parish, and the local industries; was there much poverty? He had seen the Rectory, when Mr Mallet was showing him round the estate, and thought it a well situated house; had it been her home for all her life? He did not seem inquisitive and, although he skipped sometimes from one topic to another, he attended closely to her answers. Sophia suspected that, unscholarly as he had claimed to be, he was still a shrewd quick-witted person. His easy, deferential manners drew her out into talkativeness, and she found herself describing the struggles poor Mr Mallet had had, in trying to clear the fallen elms from the Manor's avenue in time for the arrival of its owner. The story, which Sophia had had from Harry Johnson by way of Sally, had its farcical aspect, which was well received by Mr Dalby; he laughed so heartily that Sophia had to laugh too, but she recollected herself to add:

"I must not seem to mock poor Mr Mallet. He has done his best, in very difficult circumstances, to maintain all the property."

"I am sure of that," granted Mr Dalby, becoming serious. "He cannot have found much cause for mirth in his work. Indeed, when I contemplate the amount of trouble there will be, in trying to set the place to rights, I am all the more grateful for someone who can help me to see the amusing side of it."

Their laughter had attracted the attention of the rest of the party. "You are merry this evening, Miss Sophia," called Dr Jarrold. "Will you not share your joke with us?"

Mr Dalby, rising, said at once: "I am afraid I am monopolising Miss Lockley's entertaining conversation, which, all of it, I ought to share with the company." Thus sparing Sophia, and incidentally Mr Mallet, he moved to a chair beside Mrs Jarrold and began to ask her whether she and the doctor had a large family. This was well done of him, because about her sons Mrs Jarrold could be prevailed upon to talk. Her husband interrupted her at one point to call:

"I do not expect Mr Dalby is much interested in Henry's being three inches shorter than Desmond was at his age, my dear. Let Mr Dalby in turn tell you the relative heights of his own children," To which open hint, Mr Dalby responded by saying that he had no children, being not yet married.

The talk, becoming general, and under the adept guidance of Mr Dalby, filled in the evening, so that there was not need of cards or music. Sophia during the drive back to the Rectory was astonished to remember how little pleasure she had anticipated during the drive out. She tried to form her opinion of Mr Dalby. "He is clever," she decided. "He is ready to please, without being anxious to. He studies people, in spite of his tactful manner with them. He may be changeable; it is strange that he should in first sight of a place think of throwing up his business and quitting his adopted country; and it was unsteady of him to abandon his law studies and venture on anything so rash as gold-hunting. Yet he has made some success of his business; I imagine he is determined, once he sets his mind to a project, and he is energetic. I wonder how long he will be here. I should be quite glad to meet him again." So she dismissed Mr Dalby. But her enduring impression of him, which remained with her, was that he had made her laugh. He had left warmth in her spirits, because it seemed that for a very long time no one else had done so.

Thirteen

Richard Dalby was, as the members of the dinner-party had been at pains to discover, twenty-nine years old, unmarried, as yet of moderate means, well-mannered, well-disposed to this area and, in all, acceptable. He had, as Sophia had divined, exerted himself to make a good impression on that occasion, but exertion of any sort was habitual to him. He was an enthusiast, but not reckless. He was confident that he would end up by being very rich and successful, but left as little as he could to mere chance. He had set off as a younger man to Canada in the sober expectation, rather than the wild hope, of finding gold; it was he who had persuaded his friend to give up the search before it rendered them quite destitute, and he had worked very hard to insinuate them both into the fur-trading business. His inheritance from his great-uncle inevitably made him pause to reconsider his future, but it was not the easy life of a landed proprietor that tempted him; he had to calculate carefully, whether he would do better out of a well-run estate than out of a well-run fur business in

Chicago. His journey to England this summer, to visit his friends remaining in Brighton, where his aunt had brought him up, was not only on pleasure. He wanted to form some associations with fur-dealers in England and he rather wanted to find a wife. It happened that he had lately become involved with the three daughters of a solicitor in New York, and it was only because there were three of them that Richard had so far avoided committing himself. The best way out of his predicament, he reasoned, would be to return with an English wife on his arm, and present New York with a *fait accompli*. In any event, he found New York society, for as far as he had been allowed to penetrate it, snobbish and restricted, and its young ladies for the most part the same.

The new question that had now arisen – Was he to return at all to America? – superseded for the moment that of matrimony. He was genuinely attracted by his unexpectedly acquired domain and by the notion of making something of the manor-house. For this, he decided, he would like to have the advice of his friend John Goodall, the friend who had suggested purchasing the estate, and who was knowledgeable about architecture, restorations and improvements, having studied the subjects and worked on several projects before, like Richard, coming into money, whereat he had begun to look for a place to improve for his own use.

If he were to write to John, and ask him to travel north and examine the estate, however, this would take up some time. John had many social engagements at this time of year. Richard approached Mrs Mallet: for how might he trespass on her hospitality? Mrs Mallet conferred with her husband, who urged on her the necessity of doing everything possible to be friendly to their new proprietor and, Mr Mallet hoped, employer. Mrs Mallet assured

Richard that he would be very welcome to stay for as long
as he wished, and to invite his friend to stay at her house
too. So Richard, having written to John Goodall, was at
leisure as he awaited a reply, to explore his territories and
acquaint himself with the neighbourhood; about which the
news that Mr Dalby was to remain some little time among
them soon travelled.

Mr Lockley, hearing it, and remembering Sophia's
cheerfulness at the Mallets' dinner-party, decided on a
scheme that would please her. "We ought to invite the
Mallets in return," he said to his daughter, "and Mr Dalby
with them. And, since Mrs Norris says she wishes to meet
Mr Dalby, we should also invite her and Mrs Rushton. I do
not think we need invite the Williamses on this occasion.
With Robert and Lucinda, the numbers should suffice for a
pleasant party for you."

To the numbers, Sophia did not object; she even
reminded her father that they ought to include Mrs
Oldshaw in their invitation. Her hope that Mrs Norris
might meanwhile have met Mr Dalby, and uttered her
complaints to him, had not been fulfilled by the day of the
party, on whose morning Mrs Norris came to the Rectory
to give Sophia her assistance.

"No, I have not yet encountered this Mr Dalby. I may
have seen him, in the village with Mr Mallet, but he was
not presented to me. A young man, I am told. I thought
him insignificant looking. I am sure you need go to no
lengths to prepare a dinner for him, and as for my niece and
myself, as you know, we are contented with any simple
thing." Which was, Sophia reflected, as well; no pineapples
would be imported to the Rectory. Mrs Norris's assistance
this morning consisted in asking what had been ordered for
dinner, advising Sophia to change it because it would be too

costly, reminding her that she must nevertheless provide a fine meal in order to demonstrate Mr Lockley's status to a stranger, and taking herself back in haste to Ladysmead because she had pressing duties there. Sophia resumed her own pressing duties, finding them the less onerous only in that there was no one among the guests whom she wished to impress. Mr Dalby, she imagined, would not be fastidious, and she had no hope of attaining the disclaimed standards of the ladies of Ladysmead.

When the guests arrived, Mr Dalby's greeting of her, while unassuming, was so much less formal than that of the Mallets and Mrs Oldshaw that he seemed almost an old friend. He began to talk to Robert Davison about his studies, expressing admiration of anyone who could apply himself to booklearning; Robert Davison was roused to unusual animation. Lucinda, who had ridden again this morning with Mrs Rushton and was a little tired, sat abstracted, awaiting Mrs Rushton and her aunt, who came late, so late that Mr Lockley had suggested an inquiry be sent. They did at last arrive, and Sophia, who happened to be looking towards Mr Dalby at that moment, witnessed his momentary astonishment as his eyes fell on Mrs Rushton. It was swiftly concealed, but it had been evident that he had not expected to meet a lady of her style in this neighbourhood.

It was equally evident that Mr Dalby made no similar impression upon Mrs Rushton. She received the introduction coolly. Conversation between them was prevented in any case by Mrs Norris, who addressed her:

"Mr Dalby, you know, my dear, is the new owner of our house, that is, the house we are renting, and although we have not yet been told what is to become of it, or of us, you will agree with me that we are glad to meet him at last, and should take the opportunity of drawing his attention to some of the troubles we have, on account of the shameful neglect the property has suffered. I promise you, sir," turning to Mr Dalby, "we make no demands upon your time, and, from what I am told, you have no experience in dealing with such matters, but I myself am accustomed to them, and could soon explain to you what is necessary to be done. My niece and I do not expect much – we came here to live a private and peaceful life; but how can one settle to that, with indecision hanging over one, and the gutters and tree boughs blowing off at every gust of wind? I declare, to mend the wall of the garden cost me – That is, I sent the bill to Mr Mallet – but the cost was considerable, and there are many more faults to be seen to. I expect you have not yet even seen the house. You do not know which house I am speaking of."

Mr Dalby said that he had seen the house, in passing, and was sorry to hear of its condition. Moving towards the window in a casual movement of escape from Mrs Norris, he asked: "Is it not possible to see the house from here? Yes, I believe that is its chimney, above those trees."

"And more should be visible," cried Mrs Norris pursuing him, "if the trees were properly tended. From the front window of this same room, it should be possible to gain a view down towards the village, but those ash hedges and the willows by the stream have been allowed to grow wild, and it is the same wherever one goes. If you finally take over the estate – and I do not know your intentions; I hope we shall soon in informed; indecision is very trying, you know, to those in any way dependent on you – If you attempt to put the place in order, there are many small ways in which I can advise you and I shall be pleased to do so. I spare myself no exertion, in helping others. My brother-in-law, a baronet with large holdings in another part of the country, has been used to rely on me a great deal in the direction of all his affairs."

To all this, Mr Dalby replied with a bow and a murmur of: "You are very kind, ma'am." The rest of the room had become silent; Mr Mallet was quite scarlet with discomfiture. It was Mrs Norris, looking about, who rescued them all:

"But, dear Miss Lockley, is it not time for dinner to be served? It will spoil, I am afraid, if you permit your guests to linger talking for too long. Mr Dalby may tell me later what he proposes to do about his inspection of Ladysmead; we shall not let him detain us now."

Thankfully, Sophia conducted her guests to the dinner-table. This was done with no great formality, and she noticed that Mr Dalby, in the doorway purposely came near to her, to say in a low voice:

"I shall require more of your help than I expected, in seeing the amusing side of some of my new responsibilities."

Sophia had no time to answer, except with a half-smile, but that brief exchange lightened the evening for her, as did Mr Dalby's conversational adeptness. He persuaded Mr Lockley to describe the history and architecture of his church, together with that of the smaller church wherein his curate officiated, and the geography of the parish that rendered such an arrangement necessary. Mrs Norris presumed hardly at all to interrupt Mr Lockley, and the dinner meanwhile was served without incident. Mr Dalby presently said that he was much interested in architecture, and in its antiquities, of which there were very few in America, whose buildings were necessarily more modern. Mr Mallet hurried to please Mr Dalby by telling him that there were several interesting old buildings in this vicinity, such as the ruined Meldon Abbey, and that he would be happy to escort Mr Dalby to any he desired to see. Lucinda, who was still abstracted, said aside to Mrs Rushton:

"We have not yet had our ride to Meldon Abbey, have we?"

Mrs Rushton remained as silent as she had been throughout, but Mr Dalby had overheard. "You are fond of riding?" he asked Lucinda.

"Yes, very," said Lucinda with hesitation.

"Perhaps, if you wish to visit the abbey, you might accompany us, if it is not too far away?"

"Oh – I do not think so," said Lucinda, in some confusion. Mr Dalby at once made some general remark on the pleasant rides there must be, in such unspoiled country as this, and at this point Mrs Mallet, having watched the appearance of the dessert, and been reassured that there was no pineapple, made her contribution to the subject:

"I am not fond of riding myself. I prefer to go in the carriage. I do not mind the exercise, do not misunderstand me, but too much exposure to the air does not favour my complexion, if you understand me. Mr Mallet keeps a riding-horse for me, but I rarely use it. I do not care for riding."

"Then I wonder that Mr Mallet keeps on the horse," cried Mrs Norris. "It is an extravagance to feed an animal that is not used. With my small means, I have to guard against wastefulness in my own household, and although I would not deprive my niece of any pleasure, I must say, I think it almost over-generous of her to keep an extra horse, purely for Lucinda's use."

Lucinda blushed; Mr Dalby said: "That is , indeed, kind of Mrs Rushton," and asked Robert Davison whether he were a horseman.

When the company had departed, Sophia said to her sister: "You must go to bed directly, Lucie. I am sure you are tired. Did you enjoy the evening? Mr Dalby is very pleasant is he not?"

"I suppose he is. But I do not at all want to ride to Meldon Abbey with him and old Mr Mallet."

Fourteen

When Lucinda visited Ladysmead on the next morning, she found that Mrs Rushton's ideas on this did not wholly coincide with her own.

"What did you think of Mr Dalby, Lucinda?" she began.

"I did not particularly like him."

"Well, I am sorry to hear that, because my feeling is that he might do very well for you. He is not handsome, but his brown eyes are striking, and remember, he has property that may turn out to be worth much."

"Yes," said Lucinda, doubtfully. "I liked his eyes."

"Then I tell you what we shall do. We shall invite him to ride with us to Meldon Abbey. He did invite you to do so, which is a start. You should not have refused him as abruptly as you did. Men are sometimes quick to be discouraged. I do not fancy Mr Dalby is of that sort, however, and he will welcome a second chance. That old Mr Mallet can come along, if it is unavoidable, but he can talk to me while you charm Mr Dalby."

This commission turned Lucinda's cheeks pale, but she dared not defy Mrs Rushton, little as she knew herself adequate to Mrs Rushton's scheme. Maria did not suppose Lucinda adequate to it either, but she thought her plan worth trying, less from benevolence to Lucinda perhaps than from an idle impulse of spite towards Lucinda's sister. It had not escaped Maria during the dinner-party, unobservant as she was, that Miss Lockley had been very much pleased with Mr Dalby, ready for once to smile, and, in doing so, showing herself so much younger and brighter that she was positively pretty. This did not suit Maria's own discontent.

"I shall do what I can," Lucinda agreed in some anxiety. "Will you, then, write a note to invite Mr Dalby?"

"Certainly I shall not. It is for you to invite him, since it was you whom he invited. You must write the note. I myself have more important letters to write." She opened her desk to do so, wishing that in fact she had anyone in the world to write to. Mrs Norris, as Maria prepared to be busy, cried:

"Come Lucinda, leave Maria some peace, and do not be always bothering her with your own affairs. You may walk with me to the village, while Mrs Rushton is in no need of you, and help me carry back the tallow that I ordered to be left at the shop. It is a good thing I am used to exercise, and that my health is so vigorous; otherwise, I should have to send a servant for it, and they always dally about, and make an excuse for taking an hour or two over a short errand. Come along, I am ready. Let us set off at once."

Lucinda was glad to have the writing of a note to Mr Dalby deferred, though Mrs Norris by no means dallied in her own walk to the village, and the sun was hot. By chance, as soon as they entered the village, the first person they saw was Mr Dalby himself. He was with Mr Mallet, and they had paused near the pump to speak with Mr Williams, all of them on horseback. Mrs Norris exclaimed:

"Now, is that not lucky – There is Mr Dalby! You can give him your invitation immediately, and save writing. Be sure to mention that the invitation comes really from Mrs

Rushton, and give Mr Dalby her compliments. – Go along,
hurry; they may move off."

"Oh, ma'am," implored Lucinda, "would you not speak
for me?"

"Most certainly I shall not. Mrs Rushton said that it was
for you to invite Mr Dalby. Be quick about it." She waved
her hand, and caught the attention of the three gentlemen,
at the same time prodding Lucinda forward. Perforce,
Lucinda stepped forward, and timorously approached the
horsemen, who all dismounted to greet her. More
timorously, she compelled herself to address Mr Dalby, and
to say that Mrs Rushton would be happy if he would make
an excursion with her and Lucinda to Meldon Abbey.

"I should be very glad to do so." said Richard Dalby
with promptness, more out of pity for the young girl's
evident embarrassment than from any great pleasure in the
suggestion. Lucinda was emboldened to add:

"Mrs Rushton also hopes, Mr Mallet, that you will
come."

"Yes, I am sure – If there is no work I should be
attending to ... I did offer, if you remember," he said to Mr
Dalby, "to show you the ruins of the abbey. They are worth
a visit, I promise you."

"I should like to see them. Let it be arranged, as soon as
convenient, before my friend from London turns up. But,"
went on Mr Dalby to Lucinda, "is not your sister Miss
Lockley to come with us?"

Embarrassed again, Lucinda had to explain that her
sister had no horse. Mr Dalby looked disappointed; but
Charles Williams, seeing this, interposed:

"If that is all the hindrance, Miss Lockley can borrow
mine. He is gentle enough to carry her, and I can manage
for a day without him." He slapped his bay's shoulder, as if
to emphasise its placidity.

Mr Mallet thanked Mr Williams, but in the midst of doing so conceived a further idea. "That is very good of you – But, if it is a question of the lack of a horse, I am ready to promise that Mrs Mallet's could be placed at Miss Lockley's disposal. Mrs Mallet is not a keen horsewoman, and would be pleased to lend her mount to Miss Lockley. And if she does so," Mr Mallet continued, another idea striking him, "why should not you, Mr Williams, join us? Let us make up a riding party, while the fine weather holds. I hope, you can, like me, contrive to free yourself of pressing work for just one day." The outing had, originally, been Mr Mallet's idea, and he wished to make it as entertaining as possible for Mr Dalby, besides showing him that others could make space in the round of work for a day's holiday.

Mr Williams agreed to come, or at least to ride along with the rest of them for some of the distance. He mentioned that tomorrow would be a convenient day for him, and so it was decided that tomorrow should be the day, especially as some gathering clouds on the last two sunsets had begun to threaten an end of the fine spell. Lucinda engaged to invite her sister, and to explain to Mrs Rushton how the party had been formed. That it had, in the course of this present meeting, been altered from Mrs Rushton's party to Mr Mallet's did not occur to Lucinda until she and Mrs Norris, cumbered each with a block of tallow, were back at Ladysmead.

"What?" cried Maria. "We are to take Miss Lockley, and that equally dull curate, along with us? I intended nothing of the kind. The day will be quite spoilt, Lucinda. You cannot want to have your sister watching over you the whole time, as well as trying to secure Mr Dalby's attentions to herself. And how was Mr Williams allowed to push himself in? He should be more modest, in his position, than to intrude where he is not wanted. How can you have made such a muddle of it all?"

"Yes, indeed," declared Mrs Norris, "you have got everything into a sorry state, Lucinda. Poor Mrs Rushton's kind intentions are all wasted. You should have let me speak to Mr Dalby, instead of taking it upon yourself as you did. Now, Maria, your must be sadly disappointed."

"I do not know that I am. After all, I need not ride out with that crowd. Probably it will rain tomorrow, and they will be the ones to suffer the disappointment. – Of course, Lucinda, you need not mention to your sister that she is expected to go; then she will not be disappointed if we do go without her."

"But I told Mr Dalby, that I would ask her –"

"Then, forget to. Messages are often forgotten. Or persuade her that she is far too busy about the house to go out, as she often seems to think she is."

By the time Lucinda was home, she discovered that it was too late for her to be obliged to forget any messages or use any other persuasions on Sophia: Mr Mallet, acting with uncharacteristic despatch, had already had his wife send a note to the Rectory, promising that her horse would be brought there first thing next morning; which was the first Sophia had heard of any expedition. Lucinda, explaining, was upon the whole relieved that Sophia was to come, and by her presence prevent Lucinda's having to exert her charms upon Mr Dalby; at the same time, if Mrs Rushton were not to come, the repercussions on her mood, and on Lucinda, might be grievous. Lucinda did not know what to hope for, except a downpour of rain for the next four and twenty hours.

Sophia, whose invitation, as far as she knew, came directly from the Mallets, was pleased by it, and by the prospect of a change of scene, and some of Mr Dalby's company. "It will be a long ride for you," she reminded

Lucinda. "Are you sure you will not be tired?"

"No, why should I? You will probably be more tired yourself. It is a long time since you rode."

This was true, and Sophia had, in addition to rearranging the household's tasks for tomorrow, to find and air out her riding-habit. She did not seriously expect to be tired, and looked forward to the excursion possibly with more pleasure than any others of the the party, who assembled at the gate of Ladysmead next morning to wait for Mrs Rushton. It was sunny, but there was a bank of grey haze across the lower western sky that no one commented upon, though all had noticed it.

Richard Dalby was eager to see the ruined abbey, but did not entirely relish a day in this assorted company; he felt he had had sufficient socialising during the last days, and might have enjoyed the scenery in solitude. Mr Mallet was troubled as ever, lest Mr Dalby notice anything else amiss about the property; they had to pass broken fences and fallen trees along this fresh route. Charles Williams, happy to see Sophia happy, was yet privately dejected to recognise that it was upon Mr Dalby's account. Calling at the Rectory, soon after Sophia's first meeting with Mr Dalby, Charles had asked her opinion of the stranger; Sophia had given it in moderate terms, but the glow of her face as she did so told Charles that Mr Dalby attracted her. Generously glad of this, Charles was apprehensive of his own feelings on seeing the two of them together, and he was preparing excuses for quitting the party if her found those feelings too painful.

Lucinda, standing and gazing in at the gate, was dismayed that she was keeping the others waiting, and wondering what she should do if no horse were brought for her: go in and inquire after Mrs Rushton, or go quietly home? After about ten minutes of torment, she saw the groom coming down the drive, leading the grey mare, and she called to him:

"Is Mrs Rushton not coming?"

"Mrs Rushton may be coming," replied the man, making ready to help Lucinda mount. As he did so, with his back to the other riders, he gave Lucinda a wink of one eye, whose significance she could not guess.

"Shall we set off, then, do you think, Simon?"

The groom felt himself in no position to advise her, but was spared the necessity, as Mrs Rushton then approached, having mounted herself from the block, and commanded him: "Hurry, Simon, we are going. You must bring your horse and catch us up." Selecting Charles Williams as the object of her necessary greetings she said to him: "Good-morning. I suppose we may as well go, although obviously it will rain."

And she led the way, up the valley towards the moorland road they had to follow towards the abbey. Lucinda succeeded her and, as a farm cart was just them descending past them, the rest of the riders had to follow in single file, in which they continued as the lane narrowed after the cottages and wound its way up the steep woods beyond. Mrs Rushton had set a fast pace and there could be no conversation until the wider track above the woods was reached.

Before this, Sophia was experiencing difficulty. She was comfortable to be in the saddle again and the fault lay not with her equitation but with Mrs Mallet's horse, which had been too long unused, growing fat at grass, and undisciplined. It saw no reason to force itself uphill, preferring to snatch at the leaves beside the way, and would not respond to the bridle. Simon the groom sympathised, telling Sophia to give it a good taste of the whip, and offering to give the brute a thrashing for her, but Sophia hardly felt he should do so in the presence of Mr Mallet, or that she could in courtesy complain of the steed his wife had lent her. On the wider track she began to lag behind, mortified to think that she must appear an indifferent horsewoman. Simon dismounted and came to tighten the girth, saying that the horse should be less blown-out after its climb; but just then Mrs Rushton looked round to call:

"Simon, why are you hanging back? There is a gate to be opened here. Be good enough to give me your attention."

Mr Dalby, and Charles Williams, observing that Sophia was in danger of being left behind, both fell back and waited for her. Charles was concluding that he liked Dalby well enough. The man seemed to have a cheerful nature, good manners and a ready wit, and, though he showed no evidence of profound thought, that need not be expected on a pleasure trip; and he made Sophia laugh, by some allusion that Charles did not overhear. Mrs Rushton, hearing the laughter, reined back her own horse slightly, not willing to draw so far ahead that she lost all society, but complaining to Lucinda that this ride was turning out so slow, she doubted they would reach the abbey before next week.

In this way, the group proceeded along the moorland road, more or less together, Mr Mallet pointing out the scenic beauties to Mr Dalby when a tumbled wall or blocked ditch might have caught the gentleman's notice. The grey of the sky extended, and the humidity of the air caused Mr Mallet to wipe his brow with a handkerchief. Sophia's horse snorted heavily, as if falling asleep on its feet. The ground rose a little, and dipped into an area of greener fields, and Richard Dalby, not ungrateful for his agent's attempts to display the territory to him, remarked:

"Here is a farm that I suppose is not one of mine, Mallet. The walls are neat, and the hedges have been recently mended."

"Yes, Mr Dalby, your ground extends some way further. We are now at the beginning of the Ashcross Farm land, and they are excellent tenants, and do many of their own repairs."

Mrs Rushton said: "I believe you have a sister on this farm, Miss Lockley? I have seen her, running about after the geese."

If she hoped to discountenance Sophia, she was not successful. Sophia merely said that one of her younger sisters did indeed live here, and did not, although Lucinda did, look to see what effect this admission had on Mr Dalby. Claudia had been much in Sophia's mind during the ride; she was expecting her first child in a few weeks, and Sophia had not seen her for some while. She had been considering, for the last mile or so, and now said:

"I am afraid I am being so slow that I am holding you all back. It might be better, if I were to stop here, and visit Claudia, and then ride home."

This, Mrs Rushton quite approved of; but discussion broke out among the gentlemen. Miss Lockley, they agreed, could not be left to ride back alone. Mr Dalby was the most prompt to say:

"I should be happy to be presented to your sister, and to meet some of my tenants, especially such excellent ones; and then escort you home."

"But the whole point of this journey," Mrs Rushton said impatiently, "was for you to see the abbey ruins."

"If they have stood for five hundred years or so, I fancy they will not quite crumble away before I have another chance," he replied.

"I am quite capable of riding home alone," protested

Sophia. "What harm can come, in three miles of road I am familiar with?"

"That fool of a horse might refuse to budge under you," pointed out Simon.

"Simon," Mrs Rushton reproved him, "please do not favour us with your opinions until they are requested."

"I was thinking, ma'am, I should be the best one to stay with the lady."

"Well, it is not for you to think for us. I cannot do without you."

Charles Williams said: "I had intended, in any case, perhaps not to ride as far as the abbey. I can most easily turn back with Miss Lockley."

This irritated Sophia in turn. "You need not do that, Mr Williams. I shall do very well alone, and you have further visits to make, I am sure, in this direction."

Mr Mallet said: "I did not realise that the horse would be slow. It is my responsibility to accompany its rider, and Mr Williams can as well show the abbey to you, Mr Dalby."

"This is all wasting time," cried Mrs Rushton. "Are we to stay here all day, deciding what is to be done with Miss Lockley? Even at the rate she can make her horse travel, we could be a mile further on by now. I am sure the horse would not be so slow, with a more skilful rider."

Sophia could not resist suggesting in a mild tone: "Perhaps it would improve our rate of travel, Mrs Ruston, if you were to exchange horses with me?"

"I allow no one else to ride my horse," returned Mrs Rushton in a less mild tone. "Come along; let some of us, at least, move on again."

They had halted near the first barn of Ashcross, and already a row of Hodgson grandchildren was hanging along the top of a gate staring at them, and a couple of dogs had emerged to sniff the horses' heels. Sophia turning the subject looked at the sky:

"I am also afraid that the weather is worsening. It may not be possible to go as far as the abbey and back, without being caught in the rain."

"A little rain never hurts me," exclaimed Mrs Rushton.

"No? But I would rather Lucinda did not ride in it."

Lucinda said hastily: "A little rain will not hurt me, either."

"In one way or another," declared Mrs Rushton, "the day is as good as ruined. We may as well all turn back. Then you may come with us, Miss Lockley, on your nuisance of a horse, and visit your sister and her geese on another day."

Meanwhile, a short consultation had been held between Charles Williams and Mr Dalby. Charles Williams now announced: "We have settled the matter. I shall visit Ashcross with Miss Lockley, and ride home with her or not as she decides. In either event I shall be responsible for her. And Mr Dalby will go on with the rest of you, undertaking to turn back if the rain starts."

The united firmness of these two gentlemen was not to be withstood. Sophia had to let Charles Williams ride to the yard gate and unfasten it for her. As she passed Mr Dalby, she said in an urgent voice:

"Mr Dalby, you will please look after Lucinda, and make sure that she shelters, if it rains?"

"Certainly I will. Trust me."

So the party divided. Most joyful over the result of this was Claudia, to see both Sophia and Mr Williams in the yard, and to extend to them the hospitality of the farmhouse. Sophia was glad to find her sister in such good health and spirits, but her own spirits were not calmed by what she considered the officiousness of Mr Williams in undertaking to deliver her home. This was, she insisted as they prepared to leave, unnecessary.

"You need not have abandoned your excursion for me, and you are aware of it."

"I am aware of no particular regret on that score. I am sorry only for your disappointment, in having to abandon the excursion yourself."

"'I do not need your pity. Nor your company."

"I do feel, though, that the groom may be right, and that sorry jade will not bear you as far as home."

"If it will not, I will cut a switch and whip it till it does, with its owner no longer by," cried Sophia, sounding as if she would be quite pleased to do so. As Charles Williams would still not yield, she appealed to Claudia: "Do you not agree, that I am capable of moving any beast on four legs between here and the Rectory, without keeping Mr Williams from visiting Mrs Pease, or whoever may be in need of his ministrations?"

"I am sure you are," said Claudia. "But if it would comfort Mr Williams, Jethro shall saddle his pony and ride down with you. The others are all at reaping the oats, or Joseph would go with you himself."

Mr Williams, outvoted, had to be content to let Sophia ride away with the eight-year-old grandson. He watched their progress as far as the rise in the road and judged that the lazy horse might last the distance; he did not for a moment believe Sophia capable of thrashing it, despite her threats. As he turned his own horse in the direction of Brown Moss, he heard the first drops of rain rattling on the brim of his hat.

The rain began to fall on the party bound for the abbey when they had come to the end of the moor road and were dropping towards the woods of the next valley. The quartet, since Ashcross, had been as Maria had originally planned it, but she was not satisfied. The day had become dull and overcast, and Mr Mallet, whose conversation she appropriated to herself in the interests of Lucinda, bored her extremely; while, from what she could hear of the pair riding behind, Mr Dalby did all the talking, and Lucinda was not in the least trying to charm him. Bored in general, Maria began to lose interest in her scheme, and to think Lucinda an ungrateful little whey-face. For a respite, she contrived to change their positions, so that Mr Dalby rode alongside her.

This afforded Richard Dalby some relief also. He found in the younger Miss Lockley a kind of awkward coyness that did not suit her, and made her compare poorly with the wellbred young ladies of New York. Mrs Rushton too provided a contrast with them, but of a more stimulating nature. He could place her among the friends of some of his London acquaintance, or of the more fashionable visitors to Brighton, but not in this remote country. He said to her:

"You can not always have lived in the north of England?"

"I can not," she conceded, but in a forbidding tone.

"I imagine you may find life very quiet here."

"Your imagination may exercise itself as it pleases."

He took the rebuff with good grace, and told her that he himself was strange to this district, having never been further north than London. Mrs Rushton received the information without comment. His following attempts at conversation she continued to ignore or check. He had never encountered a lady so determined on not conversing with him, and he began to find it interesting.

Maria intended that he should. She had perceived, during their evening at the Rectory, that Mr Dalby prided himself on drawing people out and persuading them to talk; she would now show him that he could not always be successful. She could sense that her ruse was succeeding and that she was causing him to consider her with increasing interest, and it occurred to her that, although she still meant to attach him to Lucinda, by attracting him to herself meanwhile she would separate him from Sophia. Careless as her manner towards him appeared, Maria was careful that her coldness would not be such as to repel him, but merely to make her more mysterious to him.

A less beautiful woman would have been rash to attempt this, but to Richard Dalby, Maria's beauty was a part of her fascination, and they rode along for some time in a curious accord. It was Mr Mallet, calling to them, who drew their attention to the rain. Drops had been falling for some minutes, but now they came so heavily that all guided their horses into the partial refuge of a barn wall at the roadside.

"It is a shower," declared Mrs Rushton. "It will pass over."

"I am afraid I do not think so," Mr Mallet said.

"I am ordered by Mr Williams to turn us back when it rains," recollected Mr Dalby.

"We are not bound to obey Mr Williams. How far are we now from the abbey, Mr Mallet?"

Mr Mallet explained to her: "The road ahead of us, through the woods, brings us to the village of Hitherton at the foot of the hill. The ruins of Meldon Abbey lie about two miles on, down the river. In my opinion, our best plan would be to ride down to the village and wait at the inn there until we see whether the rain will stop."

"But if it does," said Mr Dalby, "we shall still have two miles to the abbey, and we shall probably not have much time to explore it."

"We have had too many delays," cried Mrs Rushton, "and we set out too late. It is hardly worth going on; let us turn back, as the worthy curate directed."

"We cannot turn back across the moor in this weather; look, the rain is driving now. We should make for the shelter of the woods, and for the inn, where we may dry ourselves," suggested Mr Mallet.

"Dry ourselves, in order to be wet again when we set out for home? And who could wish to waste time in a village inn?" said Mrs Rushton. "These disputes are too tedious. I shall turn for home. Come along, Lucinda."

"Miss Lockley," Mr Dalby entreated her, "I told your sister I would not allow you to get wet –"

"She is wet already," cried Mrs Rushton, "and so am I. I dare say the rain will clear if we turn back; it is the way of things."

"This has set in for the day," pronounced the groom Simon, for whose practice of speaking uninvited his mistress had already almost dismissed him.

"We do not need your opinion, Simon. Come," she said with a sudden coaxing smile to Mr Dalby, "we shall ride fast, and it is not far over the moor, and if it is still raining we can shelter at that farm where the rustic sister lives. You will see, it will be far better than going to some dirty inn, and hanging about, waiting till the rain stops, which in that case it will not. Let us turn back."

Mr Mallet still shook his head, but Mrs Rushton's smile had made Mr Dalby waver. He was not certain, so engrossed had he recently been by her interesting uncommunicativeness, exactly how far they had come from the farm where Miss Lockley and Mr Williams had left them. Perhaps it had not been too far. He acquiesced, and they rode off in the rain, back towards Ashcross. The rain did not relent. They crossed the first section of moor at a good speed, and at a bend of the road before they came to Ashcross the wind turned behind them, which kept the rain

from beating into their faces. Mrs Rushton without
drawing rein called:

"We need not stop at the farm. They would only try to
keep us, and make a fuss, and as it is, we shall be home in-half
an hour."

"But if Miss Lucinda is tired —"

"Are you tired, Lucinda?" Mrs Rushton challenged her.

"No, not at all," called back Lucinda stoutly, between
her chattering teeth. And so they went on, over the second
stretch of moor, and down the woody track into their own
valley. This took them longer than the specified half hour,
but finally they were at the gate of Ladysmead. "Ride to
your door, Lucinda; Simon, bring the mare back. Good-day
to you all," said Mrs Rushton, turning her horse in at the
gate.

Sophia was watching anxiously for Lucinda, and was
glad to see her back so early; she had been afraid Mrs
Rushton might have insisted on their pressing on to the
abbey. Lucinda told her that, on the contrary, it was Mrs
Rushton who had made them turn back; but her story was
not very full, because she was shivering and faint, and
willing to be helped to bed.

At dinner, Mr Lockley recollected: "Was it not today,
Sophia, that you were all going to Meldon Abbey?"

"We set out, Father, but because of the rain no one
arrived there."

"You should have chosen a finer day," was Mr Lockley's
reasoned summary of the matter.

Fifteen

Lucinda lay three days in bed with a feverish chill, and on every day Mr Dalby came to the Rectory to inquire after her. The truth was that he felt guilty about her. Too late he realised that he should have seen to it that she reached the shelter of the inn at Hitherton, or rested at Ashcross on the way home. He was apologetic towards Miss Lockley, whose attitude to him was cool; with cause, as he discovered on his second visit: Miss Lockley had been told that he had not wanted the riding party to turn back. He related the events of the day to her in more detail, and she forgave him.

"Mrs Rushton would not suppose that anyone else had not her own fine health," Sophia said. "And, she is apt to be impetuous."

"You find her so?" Richard Dalby asked, interested.

"I cannot truly say that I find her anything; I am surmising. She has scarcely spoken to me."

"Nor would she speak to me. She is a strange creature. Do you know nothing at all of the circumstances of her coming to live here?"

"I have not made any point of inquiring."

"And nor should I, you mean. Well, I am being inquisitive. You correct me. I must confess to you that, although I might well have called at Ladysmead to inquire whether Mrs Rushton were any the worse for her wet ride, I have not yet called at the house. You may imagine why not."

"Because you would be conducted round it by Mrs Rushton's aunt, in order to examine its disastrous condition?"

"Exactly. But I know I must face it."

"You must prepare yourself for inconceivable horrors. There is a patch of damp on a pantry wall, and a bracket has fallen off the guttering of the east end of the roof. That is all I have in fact been told of, by way of the estate mason, and Mr Mallet."

"Mr Mallet made it sound worse than that to me. Could it be that Mrs Rushton's aunt has frightened him, too?"

"I do not think, at any rate," said Sophia, "that you have."

"I? I could never frighten anyone. Mr Mallet is simply frightened of his own incompetence, but I am not sure how far he can be blamed for that. Well, I must face Ladysmead, and am thankful for your reassurance. By the way, I had a letter this morning from my friend John Goodall, who is interested in this estate; he is setting out at once from London, and he will help me to decide whether I keep the place, or sell it."

"You like it less than you did, already?"

"What I did not like," said Richard Dalby with his candid air, "was my dousing on the moor on that unfortunate day. It was a small taste of what winter could be like, in this region. On the other hand, I am inclined to treasure that manor-house, decrepit as it is. I fancy it may be made beautiful. You have been inside it? The rooms are very fine, their mouldings in particular."

"No, I have never been inside. I should like to see it."

"Then, when John is here, and Miss Lucinda is better, we shall have to make up a party to be shown round. And you can give me your opinions on what carpets and pictures it might need."

Sophia looked forward to that, as she was already looking forward to Mr Dalby's calls. She could delay her work to chat to him for an hour at a time, whereas any interruption by Mrs Norris set her whole day awry. That Mr Dalby called at the Rectory had naturally been noticed and reported. Maria wondered whether he were becoming interested in Lucinda, or whether Miss Lockley were snaring him. Charles Williams was sure that Mr Dalby, concerned as he might be for Lucinda, was attracted by Sophia. Mrs Norris thought it very offensive of the young man to come so close to their house daily and not to call. When finally Mr Dalby induced himself to face Ladysmead, her welcome was not effusive.

"We have expected you this long time," she remarked as he was shown into the drawingroom. "But in vain. You are very careless of your property, Mr Dalby."

"Technically, ma'am, between the lawyers and their probate, and my part intention of selling the property outright, I cannot feel myself in practice responsible for it."

"Responsible; aye, that is the way of it nowadays. Young people are irresponsible. That is the word I was seeking; I thank you for supplying it."

"I accept your reproof," he said; and, turning towards Mrs Rushton, who had taken no notice of his arrival: "I hope you, Mrs Rushton, took no harm from your ride in the rain?"

"And if she had," cried Mrs Norris, "she would have recovered by now, before you became responsible enough to inquire. As it happens, my niece suffered no harm, but the whole excursion was ill-conceived and foolish."

"It was an irresponsible undertaking," Richard agreed, seriously. At this, Mrs Rushton raised her eyes from her book, and directed them at him, with a coldness of non-recognition that dismayed him. Richard Dalby's pleasing manners had been cultivated on that desire, to please. He was good-natured, if calculating; but he had to be thought well of; it disturbed him to have anyone angry with him. On this occasion, he was not able to see any amusing side to Mrs Norris, who was so annoyed with him that she would not even condescend to show him the famous dilapidation of Ladysmead. Moreover, she did not wish, just now, to leave Maria for a moment alone, so alarming had Maria's mood been since that unlucky outing.

Maria would have agreed with Richard Dalby in that the weather on that day had given her a foretaste of winter; more, it had reminded her that another winter like the last lay ahead; she had been a year now at Ladysmead and felt she could bear no more of it, but saw no escape. Her depression of spirits alarmed even herself.

Richard Dalby was mistaken, then, in supposing that his unpopularity with both ladies this morning was purely personal. But in making an effort to overcome it he began to speak of the advent of his friend John, and his hopes of the manor-house. At this, Mrs Norris could not resist some admission of interest, and Richard, encouraged, let himself be drawn into offering to show her and Mrs Rushton over the house and to consult them about the carpets and pictures he might need.

"You can depend on it," Mrs Norris told him, "that with dear Mrs Rushton's exquisite taste, and my own experience and judgement, you could have no better advice, Mr Dalby, in the arrangement of your house. Let it be as soon as your friend comes, that we look over the premises. He will be as glad of our counsel."

Quitting Ladysmead, Richard asked himself whether he had contrived an occasion that could turn out altogether happily, but he decided that he would make as large a party as possible, so that he could be trapped into accepting the advice of no one person outright, and commit himself to no quick decisions. He asked Mr Mallet to see to it that the shutters were opened, the mouldering dust sheets removed from the furniture and the rooms swept out as clean as they could be. What the condition of the contents might be, he had not yet dared to ask himself; but his friend John, on first sight of the exterior, was enthusiastic.

"It is a gem," he declared, looking up from the avenue an hour after his arrival. "A perfect example of the building of that period. It must have had a good architect. There is much to be done, with the layout of the grounds, and as for the rooms – May we go in at once?"

"I am afraid the Mallets expect us to dinner. Tomorrow morning, with the neighbours I have invited, we shall make a complete tour."

The morrow was a clear sunny day of early autumn. Lucinda was now much recovered and Sophia felt it would be good for her to have fresh air and the distraction of seeing the manor-house. She had the trap brought out and sent to ask Mrs Norris if she might drive her and Mrs Rushton to the manor too, as the distance was long. Mrs Norris had of course already informed Sophia that Mr Dalby had consulted her and was relying on her advice about the planning of his house. She accepted the offer of a ride, remarking only that the trap was not large enough to convey so many persons in any comfort, but that one had to think little of one's own comfort when neighbours wished to be of service. Mrs Rushton had also consented to come, but was as silent as ever during the drive, to the evident sorrow of Lucinda.

They approached up the avenue, now roughly cleared of
its fallen elms, to see that the Mallets and Mrs Oldshaw,
and, rather surprisingly, Mr Williams and his mother, were
already here, standing talking to Mr Dalby below the steps
of the terrace, while, above, a young gentleman unknown to
them was pacing the flagstones as if measuring their extent.
Mr Dalby received the arrivals cheerfully and told them
that as soon as Dr and Mrs Jarrold were here, the tour of
the house would begin. "My friend Goodall thinks
amazingly well of it," he said. "Here he comes now – John,
let me present you to these ladies: Mrs Norris, and –"

The young man who had come running down the
shallow steps to halt before the party glanced at it out of his
preoccupation with measurements; then suddenly his face
lightened. "Mrs Rushworth!" he exclaimed in
astonishment. "How do you do?"

This was addressed, to the surprise of all, to Mrs
Rushton, whose expression altered not at all from its
normal coldness. "That is not my name, sir," she said.

"Oh, come – You must remember me? And that party on
the river at Richmond? I am John Goodall. – Surely you
remember the ball at the Frasers', when the chandelier fell?
We had some splendid times –"

"I remember nothing of you," Mrs Rushton said, with
emphasis. She turned away, adding in an angry voice:
"You are mistaken," She swept across the weedy gravel and
disappeared into a narrow path that led into the shrubbery.

Mr Goodall looked round in bafflement at everyone else.
"I am not mistaken, I am sure of that. Who could mistake
such a handsome lady? She is – or was – Mrs Rushworth,
and I knew her well when –"

Mrs Norris stepped forward, in fury. "How dare you say
you knew my niece?" she cried. "How dare you come here,
interfering, with your tales and claiming to know her well?

You know nothing. You are a liar. There is no truth in
anything you say. You have distressed my poor niece and I
will not have her upset. Has she not suffered enough? I will
not have anyone drag up the past, and spread lies about
her. You will be silent, sir. You will speak no word of your
evil slander." This was delivered in great agitation, as Mrs
Norris was in a hurry to follow her niece, which now she
did, running in her haste, parting the branches of the
unkempt shrubs with her hands, vanishing from sight and
calling out for Maria, and leaving consternation behind
her, as well as puzzlement.

Had Mrs Norris spoken more placatingly to John
Goodall, or been able to appeal to his discretion, she might
have done no harm. But her fear on her niece's account had
deprived her of even minimal tactfulness, and she had
antagonised the young man, who now announced:

"I am neither a liar nor a slanderer. That lady is Mrs
Rushworth, and she was divorced by her husband after
running away with a lover. There was a great scandal about
it in town, some while ago. We heard she and the lover grew
tired of each other and parted, and she was lost sight of.
How could I expect to meet her – and how could I fail to
recognise her? We moved in the same circles, during her
marriage, and any one of my friends in town would swear to
what I say."

It was Lucinda who broke the stunned silence that
followed Mr Goodall's speech. "*I* do not believe what you
say, sir," she cried. "Mrs Rushton is my friend and I do not
believe a word of it." She was pale and trembling and so
much affected that Sophia moved quickly to support her.
The attention of everyone was drawn to her; Sophia said to
Charles Williams:

"I must take her home. Help me with her." Mr Williams
lifted Lucinda and carried her to the trap, and Lucinda was

taken away from the scene that had disturbed her; but on all the way home she would only say: "I do not believe it. I do not believe it." She seemed not to hear anything Sophia said to her and, although Sophia persuaded her upstairs, she would not rest on her bed, but stood at the window of the room that commanded the nearest view of the chimneys of Ladysmead, gazing out in mute bewilderment.

Maria, fleeing the unwelcome revelations of John Goodall, had made her way through the shrubbery and up into the woods, to join the track along which she had ridden with Lucinda and which led back behind the village to the Rectory lane and Ladysmead. Her exposure, adding to her feelings of depression, had rendered her desperate, but in such a spirited character as hers despair seeks action rather than submission. Maria did not care in the least that the neighbourhood here should know of her past; she was frantic only, now, to escape the neighbourhood. She had to find the means of doing so.

Mrs Norris, in pursuit of Maria, did not know the track through the woods and, frantic as she was for Maria's safety, had a very painful two hours of struggling through thickets and nettles, calling her niece'e name, tearing her gown and eventually reaching home exhausted, with the idea that she must send out a search-party. Finding that Maria was safe, she was at first as much inclined to scold her for the trouble she had made her aunt suffer, as console her for the calamity of Mr Goodall's happening to know her.

"You should not have rushed away like that — The man is a liar, no one will believe him — My gown is ruined, and look how my hands are torn — We shall move to another place, my dear, and no one shall ever know you again — I always said, you know, that there was no escaping people, that all would be found out wherever we went — It is no matter, no one will care, it is so long ago, and you were in no way to blame, it was that stupid Mr Rushworth – We shall stay here, and face it out; no one will believe that wicked man –"

Maria screamed at her aunt to be quiet and leave her alone, and Mrs Norris screamed back at her that alone she would never permit Maria to be; who but her aunt had ever had her best interests at heart? Maria, who had flung herself upon the sofa, covered her ears with her hands and groaned with exasperation. At this moment, Lucinda came running unannounced into the room.

She had been able to restrain herself no longer from assuring Mrs Rushton of her loyalty and devotion, as soon as she felt strong enough after her shock of the scene of the disclosure. Dropping to her knees beside the sofa she cried:

"Dear Mrs Rushton, I do not believe a word anyone says against you, and I love you truly, and will always do all I can to help you."

Maria glanced at the girl with total indifference. "Oh, go away, Lucinda. I can not be bothered with you." Lucinda's distress irritated her; she had distress enough of her own and, besides, could imagine in no way in which Lucinda could be of value to her. Maria wanted to think, and here was simply someone else screaming at her.

Mrs Norris, quick to blame anyone for Maria's misfortunes, turned upon Lucinda at once. "Yes, go away, we do not require you, thrusting yourself upon poor Maria when she is wanting to be alone. It is no concern of yours, what has happened in the past, and you are not to come here trying to find out, and spread tattle through the neighbourhood. We wish to have nothing to do with the neighbourhood and, if you have any gratitude for all Mrs Rushton's kindness to you, you will show it by leaving her in peace and telling your sister and everyone else to do the same." As Mrs Norris said this, she was dragging Lucinda by the arm, pulling her out of the room and pushing her bodily from the house. Lucinda, weeping, had not power or will to resist.

The cruelty of her expulsion she could not comprehend. To be rejected by Mrs Rushton felt like the end of life itself. Dragging herself home, Lucinda could tell Sophia through her tears nothing except that she wanted to die.

Sophia, not wholly believing this, gave Lucinda what comfort she could, but it was late in the day before Lucinda could be calmed and would drink a little broth. She still could not explain her grief. "Come," said Sophia to her, "now you have stopped crying, try to sleep, and in the morning you will feel better, and be able to tell me all about it." But in the morning Lucinda was nowhere to be found.

Sixteen

Sophia, not wishing at first to alarm her father, set the servants and Robert Davison to search the woods and lanes in case Lucinda had merely walked out. But, apprehensive, she asked the servant whom she sent to inquire whether Lucinda had been seen in the village also to go on, and request Mr Williams to come as soon as he could to the Rectory.

Charles Williams was soon with her. "My first thought," Sophia told him in recounting the circumstances, "was that in her wretchedness she might have done herself some harm. But I would like to consult you before I explain it all to my father, because there is another thing: she has taken an amount of clothing, and, I am afraid, the money that I had put in my desk, which my father had given me to pay the tradesmen's monthly bills today. Does it not seem more likely that she has run away?"

"If she has taken money, yes. Where would she go?"

"That is what I must ask you: can she still be in touch with Peter Turner? Might she have gone to him?"

"I hardly think so."

"You have heard nothing that suggests they have written to each other, for instance? Please conceal nothing from me, this time."

"I shall conceal nothing. I know nothing. How much money was there, in your desk?" And when Sophia told him: "That would not enable her to travel far. Why should she not tell you, that she was going away?"

"That is not relevant. Except, of course, that she was evidently not herself. I think, something that was said to her at Ladysmead yesterday drove her to this. – The practical question, however, is: To what?"

Charles Williams considered. "Let us assume she was intending to travel – to her sister in Suffolk, for instance. Had she made for Ashcross, she would not have needed the money. This is market-day; she could have been given a ride to Bardton in a cart going in overnight to market. I shall go into Bardton and ask at the coaching station, where surely she will have been noticed, if she has taken a coach – a young girl, alone. If I discover in which direction she went from Bardton, I shall follow, and I quite expect that I shall catch up with her, when she has no more money to purchase further fares."

Sophia, dismayed at the picture of Lucinda moneyless in some strange town, begged Mr Williams to set off at once. He left her and she then had to tell her father that Lucinda had disappeared, but that all inquiries were being made and that Mr Williams had gone in a more extended search. Mr Lockley's anxiety was great; from all he had understood, Lucinda had caught a cold a few days ago, riding over the moor in the rain, and had been unwell. Of the crisis in her emotional life, even more than of the scandal revealed about Mrs Rushton, he had been ignorant. "And why should Mr Williams go in pursuit of her? As her father, I should have done so. He should not put himself to the expense. And why do you speak of the ponds? It is impossible that Lucinda should consider drowning herself. If so, the ponds must be dragged, not merely gazed into. I shall see to that immediately."

By good fortune, before this operation could be begun, a messenger brought to Sophia a hastily scribbled note from Mr Williams in Bardton: "Lucinda took southbound coach at 8 this morning. Following. C.W." At least, there was evidence that Lucinda was alive and that Mr Williams had some idea of the direction she had taken. But the suspense at the Rectory, as two days passed with no more news, was barely supportable. Mrs Williams came on two occasions to ask whether the fugitive had been heard of. "I expect Charles would let you know, before he wrote at all to me," she bellowed at Sophia. "So I am so bold as to apply to you. My poor Charles, he must be distracted. And your dear father, naturally."

Sophia made Mrs Williams understand that Mr Lockley had wished to go after his daughter and that she hoped Mrs Williams was not put to any inconvenience by the sudden absence of her son. "But, my dear," boomed Mrs Williams, "who but Charles should go? Let us pray he will bring her back safe. I can think about nothing else."

Nor could Sophia, but, in the district at large, the disappearance of the youngest Miss Lockley was a less enthralling topic than that of the revelation of Mrs Rushton (or Rushworth)'s scandalous history. Everyone, now apprised of this, now had always suspected that there was something strange about her; everyone was agog for a glimpse of her, in the light of the new information. Ladysmead, however, remained aloof. No one emerged, and no visitors ventured there. No one knew what to expect; so what next happened was startling enough to exceed expectation.

Maria, after a few days of tantrums and wranglings that drove her deeper into despair, was inspired from the depths of it by an idea that might resolve all her difficulties at one stroke.

Richard Dalby had meanwhile been following his friend John Goodall about, in a desultory fashion, during an extended appraisal of the domain. He was surprised to receive a note from Mrs Rushton, asking him to meet her in the summerhouse of the Ladysmead garden, approaching it direct from the upper lane, at a stipulated hour, in order to discuss a highly confidential and important matter. Curiosity prompted him to keep the appointment. If Mrs Rushton's note had surprised him, he was much more surprised by what she had to say to him.

It was towards sunset, on another clear mild day, and Richard, approaching the summerhouse as instructed, found Mrs Rushton awaiting him among the ferns of the wild garden, dressed in a simple white gown and Indian shawl, her composure greatly restored and her beauty at its most striking. She began immediately:

"Mr Dalby; I throw myself entirely on your mercy."

This was accompanied by a gaze of such appeal and brilliance that Richard felt himself almost as entirely at hers. He could only murmur that he was at her service.

Supplicant as she might be, Maria stated her case not abjectly. In the proposition she had to make she felt she would not be the only gainer. She explained, frankly, that she had committed a misdemeanour that had led to her expulsion from English society, but demanded: Was it fair that her life should be as good as ended thereby, at the age of five and twenty? Mr Dalby had seen for himself how miserable and constricted her existence in this place. Nor could she expect it to be better in any part of the country. But she had heard very well of the life in America, of its gay cities and opportunities, and was certain that Mr Dalby himself would be better suited to that background than to the dull circumstances of an English country squire. She suggested forthrightly that he decide to sell the estate and return to America with her at once.

"I confess to my indiscretions," she said in the same tone of candour, "and I shall never be tempted to repeat them. I have learnt that, in order to render life tolerable, proprieties must be observed. Hitherto, Mr Dalby, during our brief acquaintance, I have treated you with reserve. You must have perceived that. You must not imagine that it arose from any dislike of you. On the contrary, it arose from a decision I made, after the disappointments I have suffered in love, that I would never allow myself to become attracted by any man again." Without coyness, she gave Richard to understand that she did indeed find him attractive, and that the catastrophe forced upon her by his friend Mr Goodall had forced her, too, to reverse her own decision and to make this appeal to Mr Dalby.

"I am making an avowal to you," she said with her sudden smile of sincerity and charm, "and that, I know, is improper. But I make it with the most proper of intentions, and with the promise that I shall comply with you in every way, and bear you eternal gratitude, if you could find it in your heart to pity me, and deliver me from this wretched situation, and thus save my life."

Richard Dalby's natural feelings were gratified by her whole declaration, but, amazed as he was, he was not flattered out of his habitual caution. As he listened to Mrs Rushton, his calculating wits kept pace with his amazement. As naturally, he was a man of business, able to recognise a bargain when it was offered, and to seize it quickly at the same time as he weighed its possible risks. In this case, he judged that he would be fairly safe in closing with Mrs Rushton's offer. He noted that she protested no powerful affection for him, but nor had he a tenderness of feeling towards her; that was no part, on either side, of the proposed agreement. He admired her frankness, and her proper pride that allowed her to speak as she had to him without betraying her dignity. He reckoned that she was beautiful; she was the daughter of a baronet; he would have constant claim upon her gratitude; to Chicago, rumours of her past would be highly unlikely to follow her; if they did, they would cause no great stir.

For his own part, he recognised that in any case he had been losing interest in the estate recently, in proportion as John Goodall's interest in it increased; less and less could he picture himself settled here for life. Were he to sell the property and return to America with the capital it yielded, and the lovely and chastened lady now before him, he would be doing very well for himself.

"I am greatly honoured by your confidence in me," he assured her.

"Yours in me would be as great an honour, and would not, I promise you, be misplaced."

"Of that, I need no persuasion."

Without any pretence of passionate sentiment for each other, they struck their bargain with the more friendliness. Each might be serving a selfish end, but these ends coincided. The only point of dispute was that Maria insisted on being taken away from Ladysmead at once, before her nerves gave way altogether. Richard reminded her that he still had many affairs to settle with the lawyers and could not sail for America in such haste. They compromised: he would at any rate remove her from this district, perhaps to Liverpool, whence they would ultimately sail. From there, he could probably complete most of his business.

Thus their departure took place in the middle of that very night, and next day it was the news that Mrs Rushton and Mr Dalby had eloped that swept like a whirlwind through the neighbourhood.

It was certainly not from Mrs Norris that the news emanated. She had flung on the floor, for the servants to read, the brief note Maria had scrawled to her:

'I am going to America with Mr Dalby. Farewell.'

For the first time in her life, Mrs Norris's health gave way. She was utterly distraught. She lay in bed for the entire day, her head throbbing, unable to comprehend this disaster that had overtaken her.

Its effect was minimal at the Rectory, where on that same day a letter was received from Charles Williams. It was written, to Sophia's surprise, from London and addressed to her, though obviously intended also for her father. With more neatness and fulness, Mr Williams described his adventures and his intentions. He said that he had taken coach to the town of Rochdale, and there he had caught up with Lucinda, as he had hoped he might. She had already found she had not sufficient money to travel for as far as she wished, and was suffering only from the cold and her fears. She had been very glad to see Mr Williams and he had been able to draw from her an account of her conduct and feelings. She had, it seemed, been unkindly rebuffed by the ladies of Ladysmead, and had taken it very much to heart. (Here, Mr Williams interpolated that he could imagine those ladies had been in no condition just then to sympathise with their young friend, and should not be too much blamed.) Sophia wondered how much blame Mr Williams would ascribe when he heard of Mrs Rushton's elopement. The letter continued: Lucinda had told Mr Williams that she felt no one at home would be sorry for her in her loss of Mrs Rushton's friendship, because no one had liked her to be friends with Mrs Rushton anyway; and that she was not now sure that she still liked Mrs Rushton herself; there was confused mention of Lucinda's being made to flirt with Mr Dalby, which she did not think right, especially as he (here, the end of a sentence had been crossed out by Mr Williams; Sophia, studying it closely, fancied that she could make out her own name under the ink.) Lucinda, the next paragraph resumed, had explained to Mr Williams that she had the sudden desire to go to her friend Emily in Kent, because Emily would remind her of the old days when they had been happy at Ladysmead. She had run away, because she did not suppose her sister would think her strong enough to make the journey and would prevent her; she was very sorry she had taken the money and would repay it as soon as she could. The letter ended:

'She is already a little more composed, but protests that she cannot bear to return home yet. I have taken it upon myself to decide that the best thing for her would be to spend some time with the Grays. I hope this will meet with your agreement. I am taking Lucinda into Kent tomorrow, and shall then set out back north again immediately. We can discuss matters more fully when I am home.'

The arrangement did meet with Sophia's agreement; she could have thought of no better place for Lucinda to be at present than with Emily and her grandmother, and she was glad to have Lucinda away from here while the news of Mrs Rushton's escapade was creating such sensation; it might effect too painfully Lucinda's disillusionment in her heroine. It was most kind of Mr Williams, Sophia and Mr Lockley agreed, to have taken so much trouble, and they would not be able sufficiently to thank him when he returned.

Before he did, Mrs Norris had rallied somewhat. Her desertion by Maria was the greatest grief she had experienced; probably the death of her husband had less disturbed her. She regained her natural vigour, however, and came to the Rectory to voice her complaints. Sophia, relieved by the knowledge that Lucinda was in good hands, was more able to attend to Mrs Norris's woes, if not to alleviate them.

"I have devoted my life to her," Mrs Norris proclaimed. "My every waking thought has been of her welfare. And now she has cast me off. I can not bring myself to believe it. Mr Dalby made her write that note. He has seduced her. I always knew he was a wicked, evil man. Just as his friend is, who caused all the havoc. Depend upon it, they worked in league together. Poor Maria was conspired against. She is so innocent and good, she can have suspected nothing. And now she has been forcibly abducted. I have no idea where she has been taken. There is no one to help me find her. I am alone, and I have nothing now to live for. I am a sad, broken old woman." Nevertheless she mentioned, as she finally set out back to Ladysmead, that there were some ripe brambles near the gate of the Rectory that Miss Lockley had better have gathered, before the village children picked and ate them.

Sophia was able to pity Mrs Norris in her desolation and she wondered what Mrs Norris would find to occupy her solitary life. She remarked on this to her father, saying that she could not imagine Mrs Norris to be fitted for solitude; with which conjecture Mr Lockley, in his abstracted fashion, concurred.

"I expect she will leave Ladysmead now," Sophia suggested. "It is too large a house for one person, and she has no reason now to avoid society." But as to Mrs Norris's manner of leaving Ladysmead, Sophia had yet another shock in store for her.

Seventeen

Mr Lockley's pupil Robert Davison was now leaving, restored to health and well prepared for Oxford. This gave Mr Lockley the prospect of more leisure, and the relief of having Lucinda safe also disposed his mind to calm general reflection. He was not unobservant, in his way, of his dear daughters and, now that he pondered it, there had been an improvement in Sophia's looks and spirits lately, or previously to the agitation caused by Lucinda's defection. Upon further thought, Mr Lockley ascribed the improvement in Sophia to the attentions of the young man Dalby, whose character had turned out so regrettable, but who had nevertheless been an apparently pleasant and welcome companion to Sophia when he called upon her. Mr Lockley began to wonder whether Sophia might not feel life a little dull here normally, in spite of her willingness to fulfil her duties. It might be better for her to have more variety and company altogether; she might wish to visit her sisters, or even ultimately to marry. At this notion Mr Lockley flinched, but, as soon as he entertained it, he saw it as a sacrifice he should be prepared to make. When he saw his duty clear, he could not hesitate to perform it, and he decided to sacrifice himself for Sophia's sake, without at all allowing her to observe that he was doing so. His high principles forbade him even that.

As a result of his ponderings, he asked Sophia into his study, a few days after the departure of Mrs Rushton and Mr Dalby.

"I have reached a decision, my dear," he pronounced. "It will be in the best interests of all concerned. I intend to propose marriage to Mrs Norris."

Sophia, horrorstruck, could only stare.

"It may surprise you," went on Mr Lockley, unaware of how much he underestimated his daughter's reaction, "but I will explain my reasons. Firstly, she is now, as you have pointed out, quite alone. Secondly, she is an efficient and energetic lady, well able to run a household. Thirdly, she is accustomed to the duties of a parish; her late husband was a clergyman. Fourthly, she must have some income of her own, which would join with mine to the relief of our circumstances. Fifthly, it would enable you to leave domestic affairs to some extent to her, and perhaps to go more into society. I am sure you will approve my decision."

Sophia, still speechless, tried to force her stiff lips into some sort of a smile, but her father had awaited no response and had already opened a book. She left the study almost faint with shock and, in need of air, went out of doors and, scarcely knowing where she was, stood at the Rectory gate in a dazed condition, from which the sound of hooves presently half roused her. Charles Williams was riding up the lane. Seeing Sophia, he dismounted and stood looking down at her with an expression of troubled concern.

"Oh; it is you," she said in a shaking voice. "You are back?"

"I arrived this morning."

Charles had reached home at dawn, after travelling overnight, and his mother had at once brought him up to

date with the local news, the main item of which naturally
concerned Mr Dalby and Mrs Rushton. He had ridden
forthwith to the Rectory, hoping to see Sophia alone though
hopeless of offering her any comfort. This sudden encounter
caught him off his guard, as much as his sudden
appearance found Sophia off hers. Neither thought to speak
of Lucinda, although that had been Charles's ostensible
motive for his visit. Sophia's pallor and distraughtness
caused him to say with some agitation:

"I am sorry to find you so distressed, though I know the
shock to you must have been terrible."

"It has appalled me. I cannot think of anything worse to
happen."

"I wish I could help you in any way at all –"

"I wish you could. But my advice was not asked, nor
would yours be received, I am sure. His mind is quite made
up. His reasons seen to him to be excellent." Glancing up at
Charles Williams's face, she saw there some perplexity that
awoke a corresponding perplexity in herself. With more
consciousness she asked: "But how can you have heard of
it? My father told me about it only a few minutes ago. And
you have been away."

"Your father told you? But my mother says everyone has
known of it for days."

"Known that my father intends to marry Mrs Norris?"
cried Sophia.

Charles Williams's perplexity broadened into
astonishment. "To marry Mrs Norris? He has told you so?
I do not wonder you are appalled. No," he resumed, "I
knew nothing of that. I am sorry; I misunderstood. I was
referring to the affair of Mrs Rushton and Mr Dalby –"

"Good heavens, what do I care about them, in
comparison with the prospect of having Mrs Norris as a
stepmother?"

"You do not care –" Breaking off, Charles Williams with a generous effort turned his mind to Sophia's troubles. "It may be that she will not accept his offer. Has he not yet spoken to her?"

That Mrs Norris might not wish to marry Mr Lockley had occurred neither to Mr Lockley's rational, nor to Sophia's pessimistic, view of the situation. Charles Williams's suggestion offered a possibility of escape that Sophia was just now too dejected to hope for. "It is like you," she said in exasperation, "to try to be helpful when help is useless. Of course she will marry him."

"I know, I am never of any help to you."

"I do not know who could be. My life is a series of disappointments."

"It must often seem so," said Charles Williams with true sympathy. "I am very sorry. But do I understand that you are not very deeply disappointed in Mr Dalby?"

"Mr Dalby? I had no affection for him. What can have made you suppose so?"

Charles Williams had supposed so on what appeared to himself clear evidence, and for so long and so painfully that this direct question made him reply more directly than he would in a calmer moment have permitted himself. Relief at Sophia's disclaiming of affection for Mr Dalby made him say:

"I am afraid it was partly jealousy."

"Of Mr Dalby? You were jealous?" said Sophia, failing to understand. "Why in the world should you be jealous of anyone?"

She seemed genuinely not to know; her detachment, strangely, gave Charles Williams the courage to betray himself, and a reckless desire to declare his feeling and make an end to the matter. "Because I love and admire you more than anyone I have ever known, and have done so ever since I knew you." As she stared at him, still not comprehending, he hurried on to commit himself beyond retreat: "And, if you cannot bear the prospect of living with Mrs Norris in the family, which I can fully sympathise with, let me offer you an escape by asking you to marry me."

Sophia's response to this was immediate laughter. "Charles," she cried, unwittingly addressing him by his Christian name, "you cannot be so absurd as to want to marry me just to rescue me from Mrs Norris. Nor can you possibly be fond of me, when I have made myself as disagreeable as I could to you, on every occasion, and you can only think me a bad-tempered and selfish old maid – which I am."

"You are not," said Charles. "And I love you."

The gentleness and simplicity with which he said this made Sophia look up into his eyes, and what she saw there made her own eyes suddenly fill with tears. A strange, wild hope leapt up in her.

"If only I could believe you," she said in a whisper.

"Please believe me."

What Sophia had seen was that Charles forgave her. In his forgiveness all her crossness and selfishness melted away and dissolved in his love; she was renewed, lovable. Contrition gave her an impulse towards him that made her cry: "Oh, Charles, how wonderful it would be to be loved by you, because indeed I have loved you too, and I have relied so much on your patience and kindness, and I have been so ungrateful, and deserved none of it, and I knew that, and that is what has made me so disagreeable to you, and I am sorry, so sorry, and if only I might be with you I could be happy and behave better and love you all my life."

She wept with remorse and joy, each enhancing the other. To be comforted by Charles made up for all her years of loneliness. She felt only that she had wasted so much of her life in fretting over difficulties that she had brought upon herself, ignoring Charles's existence; now, the past had dissolved like a bad dream.

Charles was too bewildered by the completeness of her surrender to him. They walked to and fro in the lane for some time, to calm their spirits and enjoy their newborn understanding. Presently Charles asked:

"May I speak to your father?"

"Oh, please. Please do, directly. I do not care about Mrs Norris now. Except that I am sorry for poor Father. Shall you make it a double wedding – you officiating for him, and he for you?" said Sophia, fully restored to cheerfulness.

"I am afraid you may find my house too small, Sophia," said Charles restored to some sense of the mundane. "And, as you are well aware, my mother is not easy to deal with –"

"Oh, yes, she is. I love her dearly. I shall soon find out how to pitch my voice, as you do, so that she may hear me better. But will she be pleased to have me? I have fancied that she wanted you to marry Lucinda."

This amazed Charles. Reminded, they went on to talk of Lucinda, and Sophia had to hear again all the tale of his finding and escorting her. Mr Lockley had still to hear it; they decided that, since he would wish to hear it at once, Charles could not keep from him his request for Sophia's hand, and the two interviews could be combined. Charles went to knock at the door of Mr Lockley's study, and Sophia was left to reflect that, if her father had given her a shock this morning, she was probably retaliating only a couple of hours later.

Mr Lockley was considerably surprised to be told that Sophia and Mr Williams wished to marry, but he could not but consent. He held Mr Williams in very high regard and could not have hoped for a better husband for his daughter. Only, later that evening, he said after long thought:

"I had no idea, Sophia, that you were so fond of Mr Williams."

"Nor had I, Father," replied Sophia. The reply puzzled Mr Lockley, but since Sophia was so noticeably improved in looks and spirits all at once, he could have no doubts of her happiness.

It did occur to Mr Lockley that, with Sophia living nearby, and settled, perhaps he need not proceed with his plan of proposing marriage to Mrs Norris. He dismissed this retraction as unworthy. He had conceived of his plan as a duty, and, as such, it was not to be shrunk from. He took twenty-four hours to consult his conscience, but as usual his conscience prevailed. Gloomily, he requested Sophia to have his best suit and new boots set out for him an hour after dinner in the evening. Sophia could well guess why, but Sally could not.

"Why should the Master want his new boots at that time on a weekday?" Sally asked in the morning as she and Sophia took the suit from its closet. Sophia dared not yet tell her. The installation of Mrs Norris at the Rectory would inevitably lead to the ejection of Sally, who would them presumably have to be accommodated in the Williamses' house. This prospect did little to mar Sophia's present happiness, but she did not know that it would appeal to Sally. Sally, delighted as she was that Sophia was to marry Mr Williams, had already commiserated with her for having to live with 'that shouting deaf lady'.

"I expect he has a visit to pay," Sophia half-explained. "See that the boots are well polished, pleased."

"I shall put the suit in the air for a while, as it's warm," Sally said. Laying the coat across the sill of the open window of Mr Lockley's bedroom she exclaimed: "Now, that looks exactly like that young man that ran away with Mrs Rushton, or whatever they call her. Well, it can't be.

He would never have the effrontery to show himself in these parts again."

Sophia, moving to the window, saw, with eyes younger than Sally's, that Mr Dalby himself was riding up the lane, quite at his ease, glancing about him as if to admire the autumn colours of the trees. Before Sophia could draw back from the window his glance had passed in her direction, and he saluted her with his riding-whip and entire composure.

"Good-day, Miss Lockley," he called. "I trust you are well?"

She could only call back: "Yes, I thank you."

"May I visit you presently, if you are at liberty? I am on my way to call at Ladysmead, but should be pleased to speak to you after that."

If he survived his encounter with Mrs Norris, Sophia would not be displeased to hear what he had to say for himself; and, more particularly, why he was calling at Ladysmead. She supposed she must receive him, as he had so politely asked if he might call; curiosity overcame scruple. Nor had she to contain her curiosity for long. It was only about half an hour after he had ridden up the lane that Mr Dalby presented himself to the door of the Rectory.

Sophia greeted him with: "You were only a short while at Ladysmead."

Mr Dalby laughed. "I was almost flung out, by Mrs Norris's haste to start packing."

"She is going away?" asked Sophia on a note of hope.

"I am taking her with me to Liverpool. Do not look astonished; are you among those who believed Maria and I had formed an illicit union? I received some very outrageous looks as I rode through the village, and Mrs Norris had – not unreasonably I suppose – suspected me of that and worse. But I promise you, I conducted Maria in complete propriety to Liverpool, where she is established at present in a respectable lodging. Now that she is delivered from this distict, her nerves are marvellously recovered, and I am glad I took her away as quickly as I did. Otherwise, she might have quarrelled with her aunt past mending. As it is, she has forgiven her, and desires her to travel with us to America when we go."

"I hope that is what you desire," said Sophia with caution.

"Oh, well, she knows Maria's ways, and will bear her company if I have to travel about on my business. If Maria wants her, I am content. Maria and I are to be married, by the way, in a civil ceremony, before we sail. Mrs Norris was much reassured to hear of that, and insists on witnessing that the ceremony actually takes place. I am not sure that she yet altogether trusts me."

Sophia wondered whether Mrs Norris might not be justified in that, but she could be relied on to watch over her niece's interests and must have been overjoyed at the restored opportunity of doing so. Sophia was joyful too, and exclaimed: "I must tell father of this, as soon as I can."

Falling into her easy habit of chat with Mr Dalby, she was indiscreet enought to explain why. Mr Dalby cried:

"Then you must look upon me as your deliverer!"

"Indeed, I am not ungrateful. And I wish you, all three, every happiness."

When Mr Dalby returned the good wishes, she had to mention to him how those wishes were to be fulfilled, and he congratulated her warmly. "I admire Mr Williams. I found him a steady, sensible man; but I was not always sure that you yourself valued those qualities in him."

Blushing, Sophia said: "You are too acute."

"Yes, and I am impertinent. You must forgive me. Think of me, often, when you see what a splendid affair John

Goodall makes of this estate, and rejoice that I am not here to make a worse job of it."

Sophia undertook at any rate to think of him; they parted amiably. Then she summoned the courage to go straight to her father and break it to him as gently as she could that he was to lose his bride.

Mr Lockley was, as ever, inscrutable; from his reception of the news Sophia could not gauge the depth of his disappointment, but he appeared to support the blow courageously.

Behind his inscrutability, Mr Lockley was at some pains to conceal his relief. He told Sophia: "You may put away my new boots. I may not need them until the day of your wedding."

Eighteen

Maria herself could not have been more impetuous than Mrs Norris in her desire to be rapidly away from Ladysmead. Before Mr Dalby came back for her with a carriage she spared only a few minutes to make her farewells at the Rectory, or to exult in her release.

"All is happening in such a hurry, my dear Miss Lockley, I declare I have no time to think. I shall take with me the bare necessities and leave the rest to be sold up. Mr Mallet can see to it. I shall just have to trust him, and if Maria's father wants the pianoforte, why, he must send for it, I cannot be bothered by details. By the way, Nanny says you are to be married, and I wish you well. It is a pity about Nanny, who has been for so many years with me, but I shall give her what money I can spare, and she can tidy up the house and then find her way back to our original home. I shall have to trust her: I have never in my life had to depend so on others, but there is no help for it. Maria needs me, and I must go to her at once."

Maria had, as Mr Dalby reported, relented towards her aunt, as soon as she had escaped her. When they were reunited in Liverpool they soon began to bicker as much as formerly, but Maria was at heart a little nervous of

venturing so far overseas with no companion she was used
to. She soon heard from Mr Dalby that Mr Lockley had
intended to propose marriage to her aunt; without
communicating this to Mrs Norris, Maria consoled herself
a little with the possibility that she might yet marry Mrs
Norris off to some suitor in America if her aunt's presence
proved unnecessary to her there.

Most of what Maria' had told Richard Dalby in the
summerhouse was true: she was resolved to avoid all
indiscretions and to be a loyal wife; she did, having resolved
on this too, find him personable enough as a man. The two
of them got along well enough, and indeed grew quite fond
of each other, agreeing in a fundamental coldness of heart
and a high value of outward appearance. In New York, and
later in Chicago, Maria's connections with the English
aristocracy were well regarded, and admitted them into the
best society. In these strange surroundings Maria was not
too proud to have a husband engaged in trade, and, as
Richard's business affairs prospered, their style of life was
as elegant as she could wish. She was glad to have a
husband so unlike her first, whose stupidity had bored her
to distraction; Richard remained pleased with his wife's
beauty and social charm; although Mrs Norris remained
unmarried, she was useful in that Mr and Mrs Dalby vented
upon her the irritation they might otherwise have turned
towards each other. Their household was not an unhappy
one.

In England, Sophia and Charles were married by Mr
Lockley at Christmas. Lucinda did not travel up from Kent
for the occasion. Her health was improving, but it was
thought better to leave her for a while in the tranquil
company of Mrs Gray and Emily. Mrs Gray wrote to
Sophia that at first Emily and she had found Lucinda
much altered, with some strange ideas and manners; but

that she had begun to resume her interest in reading and music, and to show gratitude for her friends' affection for her. Perhaps when spring came, Lucinda would be more like herself again, and ready to return home.

Before the spring, Sophia and Charles were settled in Ladysmead. This had been John Goodall's idea, because he protested he did not know what to do with the house and had enough problems with the rest of the estate for the meantime. The rent would be nominal; it was merely that he wanted the house to be occupied. Sophia was delighted to move to Ladysmead; she had always admired the house, and it was certainly more spacious than the Williams cottage. Her only objection, that it would mean Charles's living at a greater distance from his church, Charles readily dismissed. Mr Lockley too was pleased to have his daughter and his curate so close at hand.

John Goodall proved an efficient landlord and by degrees made a splendid home of the manor-house. When he married, his wife's friends and his own, constantly visiting, added greatly to the society of the neighbourhood. Sophia sometimes wondered that she had ever thought life dull here.

Lucinda returning north spent more time at Ladysmead than at the Rectory, and there was coming and going between Ladysmead and Ashcross. Mrs Williams, removed to Ladysmead, found occupation in making herself useful at the Rectory and was constantly trotting to and fro across the lane to keep an eye on Mr Lockley. Her deafness, more pleasantly than Mrs Norris's officiousness, forced Mr Lockley out of total reclusiveness; unable to make her hear that her attentions were not always necessary, he had to become resigned to them, and became reliant on Mrs Williams; not, however, to the point of proposing matrimony. He no longer saw this as a duty, since they all seemed quite happy as they were; and so they remained, although no efforts that were made, throughout the years, ever quite obliterated one small damp patch from the pantry wall of Ladysmead.